Hearts Don't Lie

Book Six, MacLarens of Fire Mountain
Contemporary Western
Romance

SHIRLEEN DAVIES

Books Series by Shirleen Davies

<u>Historical Western Romances</u>

Redemption Mountain
MacLarens of Fire Mountain Historical
MacLarens of Boundary Mountain

<u>Romantic Suspense</u>

Eternal Brethren Military Romantic Suspense
Peregrine Bay Romantic Suspense

<u>Contemporary Western Romance</u>

MacLarens of Fire Mountain Contemporary
Macklins of Whiskey Bend

The best way to stay in touch is to subscribe to my newsletter. Go to my Website *www.shirleendavies.com* and fill in your email and name in the Join My Newsletter boxes. That's it!

Avalanche Ranch Press, LLC
PO Box 12618
Prescott, AZ 86304

Book design and conversions by Joseph Murray at 3rdplanetpublishing.com

Cover design by Sweet 'n Spicy Designs

ISBN: 978-1-941786-20-8

I care about quality, so if you find something in error, please contact me via email at shirleen@shirleendavies.com

Description

His artless proposition should have ended it. What does he do now when she refuses to back down?

Mitch MacLaren has reasons for avoiding relationships, and in his opinion, they're pretty darn good. As the new president of RTC Bucking Bulls, difficult challenges occur daily. He certainly doesn't need another one in the form of a fiery, blue-eyed, redhead.

Dana Ballard's new job forces her to work with the one MacLaren who can't seem to get over himself and lighten up. Their verbal sparring is second nature and entertaining until the night of Mitch's departure when he surprises her with a dare she doesn't refuse.

With his assignment in Fire Mountain over, Mitch is free to return to Montana and run the business his father helped start. The glitch in his enthusiasm has to do with one irreversible mistake—the dare Dana didn't ignore. Now, for reasons that confound him, he just can't let it go.

Working together is a circumstance neither wants, but both must accept. As their attraction grows, so do the accidents and strange illnesses of the animals RTC depends on to stay in business. Mitch's total focus should be on finding the reasons and people behind the incidents. Instead, he finds himself torn between his unwanted desire for Dana and the business which is his life.

In his mind, a simple proposition can solve one problem. Will Dana make the smart move and walk away? Or take the gamble and expose her heart?

Hearts Don't Lie, Book Six in the MacLarens of Fire Mountain Contemporary series is a full-length novel with an HEA.

Hearts Don't Lie

Prologue

Crooked Tree, Montana

"I don't know what you want. You dump this on me, on the entire family, and expect us to accept it without complaint. Fine." Mitch MacLaren, Rafe MacLaren's second oldest son, placed fisted hands on his hips, his face reflecting the anger and resentment boiling inside. "I'll do my best, but there'll be no open arms coming from me." He stormed toward the door, grabbed the handle then stopped. "I'll be in the back corrals with the stock manager." The walls shook with the impact of the slammed door, rocking the family photos and business awards collected over many years.

Rafe would've followed him, except he knew Mitch better than most. Father and son were alike in many ways, some good and some bad, which often triggered their explosive interactions. This time, however, Rafe could understand Mitch's hurt and anger. He knew firsthand how a father's actions could impact loved ones years after the fact, changing futures and ruining relationships.

He grabbed his desk phone on the second ring. "Yeah...okay, thanks. Tell him I'll be right down." Lowering the phone, he wondered if any solution would satisfy all those he'd hurt.

Rafe took the stairs to the ground level slower than normal, forcing calm to replace the agitation his conversation with Mitch caused. He almost laughed at the absurdity of the thought. Calm had eluded him ever since he'd stormed into the old homestead, the MacLaren ranch house in Fire Mountain, Arizona, demanding his estranged brothers back off from their acquisition of his bucking bull rodeo stock business. The room had been full of family, relations he'd never met and cared nothing about. Not only had Heath and Jace refused to withdraw their offer, but a man he'd never met had the nerve to confront him, tell him he was a fool if he didn't take what amounted to a once in a lifetime deal to secure the business for his family.

He could still feel the shock and pain in his gut when he learned the man's identity—a son he'd never met, didn't know existed until that minute.

Kade Santiago Taylor MacLaren now waited for him downstairs, not interested in taking his place as the oldest son in Rafe's family, but at least willing to meet his father partway. It was more than Mitch could offer.

"Kade." He held out his hand. Pulling him into a hug seemed inappropriate. Perhaps someday.

"Hello, Rafe." Kade clasped his hand, not moving from where he stood near a large picture window opening toward the stockyard.

"How was the trip?"

"Uneventful, except for this." He held up the cane he'd been forced to use since his accident a few months before.

Rafe turned to the receptionist. "Call Mitch and the others. Let them know Kade's here. Are you okay with stairs?"

Kade nodded, following Rafe to his office.

As with the lobby area, full length windows provided a view to the stockyards as well as the rolling hills beyond. Rafe pointed to a picture on the wall, then faced Kade.

"This was taken a couple of years ago. Mitch, Sean, and Rhett, who you will meet in a minute, and Skye and Samantha." He pointed to his three other sons and two daughters. "The girls will be at dinner tonight."

"Heath said you're getting divorced." Kade looked at the image of the woman Rafe had married, the mother of the brothers and sisters he had yet to meet.

"It's been coming for a long time. She lives in San Diego now. She never did care much for this way of life." He shrugged, not indicating how he felt about the breakup of his marriage. "It should be final within a couple months."

"Hey, Pop." Rhett walked in followed by Sean and Mitch.

Rafe shot a wary glance at Kade, noting his total lack of emotion at the sight of his half-brothers.

"There's no easy way to do this. I've already explained as best I can. Now it's time the four of you met."

Rafe introduced the sons he'd raised to Kade, the oldest of the four, who'd never shared their life.

All went well until Mitch stepped forward. He eyed Kade, his gaze not wavering while he took in his older brother, measuring him against the image he'd developed. Their father had taken his other kids aside earlier that week, explaining what happened almost thirty years ago, and in no way apologizing for dropping a bombshell on his family. Kade was now the oldest MacLaren son, changing the dynamics of the family in a heartbeat.

Rafe watched Mitch openly evaluate Kade, deciding how he'd react and if he'd accept him. What Mitch did or didn't do would have a huge impact on whether the others brought Kade into the fold.

Mitch held out his hand, not in welcome, but in acceptance of a fact he couldn't change.

"Kade." One word, that's all Mitch offered as the two shook hands. Kade was an outsider, an interloper, no matter what his father said. This measure of civility was all Kade would get until he proved himself worthy to be called a MacLaren.

Chapter One

Fire Mountain, Arizona
Six months later...

Mitch packed the last of his personal belongings into the box and looked around. He didn't bring much with him from Montana when he arrived six months ago. He hadn't expected his assignment at the MacLaren Enterprise's headquarters to last this long, thinking he'd be back in Crooked Creek within weeks. None of the company leadership—Heath, Jace, or his father, Rafe MacLaren, agreed.

Not until the last two weeks, as he prepared to leave, did he understand and appreciate what he'd learned over his stint at the corporate headquarters. Mitch thought he knew most of what there was to know about running a company. He'd been dead wrong.

Unlike RTC Bucking Bull Stock, the company his father and two partners started, MacLaren Enterprises included multiple companies in various states. Businesses ranging from cattle ranching to land acquisition and development to bucking horse stock and specialized horse breeding. In six months he'd learned not nearly enough, but the time had come for him to take his place beside his father until Rafe fulfilled his promise to relocate to Fire Mountain as one of the key executives—at least for two years. Heath and Jace wanted their brother beside them, fulfilling their father's dream of having all of his sons run the dynasty he'd begun.

"Need any help?"

Mitch looked up to see Eric Sinclair, a relative by marriage and good friend, assess the state of the office.

"Nah, there's not much to pack. I've already sent a box of files north. Guess I'm old school as I prefer to hold paper than read everything on a computer screen."

"I hear you. When do you start back?"

"Tomorrow morning. Figured I'd get you and Kade to help me load the Harley in the back of my truck tonight after dinner."

"Guess the whole tribe will be at Mom and Heath's tonight for your farewell meal." Eric's mother, Annie Sinclair, had married Heath MacLaren several years before, creating a dynamic and tight-knit family.

Mitch snorted. "Hell, it's not like I'm dying or going away forever."

"Although there are days I bet you wished you could leave us behind and never look back."

"Damn straight. Seems I'm not the people person the rest of the MacLaren-Sinclair clan is."

"Maybe not, but you do pretty well." Eric picked up a framed picture sitting on the top of the box and looked at each of the faces. Taken at his and Amber's wedding, it showed all the MacLarens and Sinclairs, including spouses and close friends. The wedding occurred a few weeks before, yet it had taken the two of them a long time to find their way back to each other after years apart. He held it up.

"This has to be the best picture ever."

"That it is, bro."

Eric laid it back in the box. "Drinks at The Tavern before we all head over to the ranch house."

"I'll be there."

Mitch watched the door close, a strange sense of melancholy gripping him. He'd never been the sentimental type, and if anyone accused him of being torn about leaving Fire Mountain, he'd have called them a liar. He couldn't deny he'd miss the place and the way everyone huddled together at the sign of trouble.

******

Kade walked into the bar, the place he and his buddies hung after work or for sport events when they weren't congregating at one of the houses or cabins. He glanced at the bartender who nodded toward the corner where Mitch, Eric, and Cameron, Eric's older brother and president of the MacLarens' bucking horse business, already huddled around a table.

"About time," Eric said as Kade stopped next to Mitch.

"What'll it be, Kade?" The waitress let her gaze wander over Mitch as she waited for Kade's order.

"Beer. Actually, bring another round for the table."

"Will do." She shot a smile at Mitch before sashaying toward the bar.

"Isn't that the girl you met at the wedding?" Cam asked Mitch.

"Yeah. She came with a friend." He glanced around the bar, seeing a number of people he recognized.

"Amber mentioned you took her out a couple times." Eric watched as the waitress set Kade's beer on the table.

"No big deal." Mitch shrugged, watching as she left the group to themselves. Drinks, dinner, and bed—what they had both wanted.

"Dana seemed to think it was a big deal." Kade sipped his beer, keeping his expression blank. He and Mitch had come a long way in the last few months, forging at least somewhat of a bond if not quite the relationship the rest of the family had hoped.

"Dana can keep her thoughts to herself. She's got a big mouth and is nothing but trouble." Mitch downed his whiskey, signaling the waitress for another. "I heard Heath may offer her a job. Don't know why when they get her services cheap as a contractor."

"Loyalty, Mitch. The brothers put a lot of stock on loyalty and surrounding themselves with those they can count on."

"The brothers? Is that what we're calling Heath, Jace, and Rafe?" Mitch scoffed.

"It's what Mom calls them—to their faces," Eric answered as the waitress set down another round.

"I get the loyalty thing. It's just, I wonder what she can offer as an employee that she isn't already providing as a contractor." Mitch tilted his glass up, taking a long swallow.

Kade narrowed his eyes at Mitch, not understanding why the situation irritated him so much. Amber's friend, Dana Ballard, had lost her job in Denver and relocated to Fire Mountain for a new start. She worked three jobs to make ends meet, never complained, and did excellent work. Plus, she'd shown her mettle during some tough times involving Kade's former job as a DEA Special Agent.

"What's your problem with Dana anyway? Seems you've been on her since she arrived from Denver." Kade kept his voice neutral, even though Mitch's surly attitude got to all of them at times.

"I've been on her?" Mitch snorted. "That woman's been a pain in my ass since she arrived. Bossy with a smart mouth and never stops asking questions. Drives me nuts."

The others shot amused looks at each other. They'd heard his grumblings about Dana before and not one believed it rose to the level Mitch wanted them to believe. In fact, they'd lay odds on the opposite. Funny and upbeat, Dana's personality couldn't be more opposite Mitch's brooding, stoical nature.

"I sure hope you can keep your opinions of her to yourself tonight." Kade set his empty glass on the table, then leaned an arm on the edge.

"Why is that?"

"Because Annie and Heath invited her to dinner," Kade answered.

"Ah hell. She's not family. There's no reason she

should be there." Mitch signaled for the check.

"I wouldn't worry too much about it. My guess is she's going to be as glad to see your taillights as you'll be to pass Fire Mountain city limits. Perfect solution." Cam tossed back the rest of his drink and grabbed the check. "Now, let's go get some food so we can say goodbye to your sorry ass." He slapped Mitch on the back, not nearly as ready to see him depart for Montana as his words implied.

******

"Come on, spill. Who is he?" Amber's brows flickered up and down at the same time she used a tortilla chip to scoop up a large serving of guacamole. "I heard he's pretty, well, amazing." She laughed, stuffing the chip in her mouth.

Dana Ballard didn't take the bait. She'd had one date with a new addition to the local search and rescue team. Cam and his wife, Lainey, both members of the town's SAR group, met him while attending one of the monthly meetings.

"We've gone out once, and that was a double date with Cam and Lainey."

"And?"

"And what? He seems like a nice guy, attractive, smart, built. You know, your basic average guy." Dana laughed, knowing average didn't begin to describe the hunk Lainey had convinced her to meet. "He called this morning. Wants to go out this weekend, but I don't know."

"What's not to know? You haven't dated since you arrived in Fire Mountain. All you do is work, go to the gym, ride your bike, and hang out with me." Amber handed her a chip already loaded, watching as Dana crammed the whole thing in her mouth. "How about Eric and I go out with you and...what's his name?"

Dana took a sip of diet soda, washing down the remnants of the corn chip and swallowing. "Kell Corwin. He's a county prosecutor."

Amber almost choked. Dana had a long standing aversion to attorneys or those in law enforcement. She never understood her reasons for avoiding certain men, but it had been the same when they both lived in Denver.

"Wow. That's new for you."

"What's new?" Cassie MacLaren, Heath's daughter, snatched a chip out of Amber's hand. "What did I miss?"

"Dana's started dating."

Cassie's eyes widened at the unexpected news. "No kidding. Who is he?"

"Who's who?" Kade walked up with his wife Brooke, and Mitch.

"Geez, this is getting out of control," Dana complained, although her smile didn't fade. She drained her can of soda while slipping her gaze to Mitch, hoping he didn't catch her staring.

"We're talking about the hot new man in Dana's life," Cassie added. "Now, who is he?"

"Not that it's anyone's business, but it's Kell Corwin. Cam and Lainey introduced us."

Mitch shifted his stance, crossing his arms while planting his feet shoulder width apart, his gaze narrowing on Dana.

"No kidding? I heard he's about the most eligible bachelor in town. An attorney, right?" Brooke asked.

"Yes, he is. A county prosecutor. Transferred up here from the valley a few months ago."

"And a real hunk," Cassie added, looking at the amused faces of the others. "What? That's what I've heard."

"So, is he, Dana? A hunk?" Amber asked, noticing Dana's face color.

Dana crossed her arms and glared at Amber. "All right. Here's the deal. He's about six feet tall, so buff he strains his shirtsleeves, has tawny blonde hair, a tan to die for, a great smile, and a killer laugh. Oh yes, and he's smart, funny, and a volunteer with the local SAR team. Anything else?"

Kade coughed, trying to stifle a laugh. "So when are you having his children?"

Everyone, except Mitch, laughed. He continued to watch as Dana's laughter stilled, his jaw working, although he remained silent. Something about her meeting and dating someone bothered him in a way he couldn't understand. He should be glad. Although after tonight, nothing about her would matter one way or another. The odds were he'd never see her again once he left for Montana—and he couldn't get away soon enough.

"Dinner's ready." At Annie's announcement, the

crowd moved to the large dining table. All except Dana and Mitch.

"Blonde, buff, with a killer laugh, huh?" Mitch smirked.

"Yeah, well, it's better than dark and surly." She slid a strand of red hair behind her ear before slipping by him toward the food.

He stared after her, shaking his head. No matter his personal feelings about her, at least he never had to wonder what she thought. They were like oil and water, or fire and ice as Kade once said. Regardless, it would be a cold day in hell before they'd ever have a civil conversation.

******

"She's secure." Kade tested the last tie-down holding the Harley upright in the back of Mitch's truck. "You going to drive straight through?"

"That's my plan." Mitch glanced at his watch. Almost midnight. He'd get a few hours of sleep, then hit the road. Even though he hadn't been thrilled with Annie's idea of having the family over to say goodbye, he had to admit, the evening went well. Except for one overbearing redhead, he'd miss each one.

"Have a safe trip, man." Kade held out his hand. "Don't forget to write," he smirked when Mitch grabbed it in a firm shake.

"You'll be lucky to get an occasional text message."

The two spun on their heels to see Dana a few feet away holding a small box. Mitch thought everyone except Eric and Amber had left, including the vixen standing before him.

"You still here?"

"Don't shoot the messenger, big guy. I'm delivering a care package Annie put together for the road." She set it on the hood of the truck, noticing Kade pull out his keys.

"I'm out of here. Keep in touch." Kade gave a mock salute before climbing on his bike and maneuvering out of the gravel drive, leaving Mitch to deal with the firecracker he most wanted to avoid.

He didn't know what about Dana set him off. They'd been at each other from their first encounter months before when Amber introduced them. Brash, creative, and straight forward, she hadn't let his brooding manner stop her from poking at his life, asking questions, pushing all his buttons. They bickered like siblings who'd grown up together, except his body's reaction to her had nothing to do with brotherly affection. Far from it, and that was the main reason he never let her get too close.

Red hair had never turned him on, nor had outspoken women. He preferred brunettes with soft curves, warm smiles, and open arms that knew when to let go. Mitch had the feeling if Dana ever got her claws into a man, it would be all over except for the sounds of surrender. From her description of Kell Corwin, she may have found someone to keep her occupied for some time. The knowledge didn't give him any comfort. He moved toward her, taking the box off the hood of the truck and stowing it on the seat next to him, then turned to look at her.

"Have a safe trip, handsome." Her blue eyes sparkled in the moonlight, although he could detect a look of what? Melancholy...regret?

"No goodbye kiss?" he half-teased.

Her gaze narrowed on his, her lips set in a thin line as if she struggled with a decision. "Sure, why not." She rose up on her toes, placing what was meant to be a peck on his cheek.

In a quick move, Mitch wrapped his hands around her arms, pulling her tight as he shifted, his mouth finding hers. The kiss was demanding, coaxing, the intensity sucking all the air from her lungs. She pulled her arms free, wrapping them around his neck, drawing him down as their tongues collided, tangling, as if fighting for dominance. He set his hands on her waist, dragging her closer, taking everything he could as heat flared between them. Letting his hands roam up and down her back and hips, he grabbed her shirt, intending to pull it free. Instead, her moan snapped him out of his passion-induced trance. As quick as it started, he set her aside, his breath ragged.

"That was some goodbye kiss, lady." His voice unsteady and husky, he dropped his hands, shoving them in his pockets so as not to reach out and pull her back.

She dragged in a breath, not meeting his gaze, giving herself time to calm down from what had been the most remarkable kiss of her life. But she sure as hell would never tell him.

"Yeah, well, don't expect the same next time, cowboy." Her hands fidgeted at her sides before she clasped them in front of her, finally crossing her arms over her chest. "Don't run out of gas," she quipped, then turned and stalked toward her old Jeep, her heart still pounding in her throat. At least her breathing had returned to normal...almost.

Mitch's hooded gaze stayed with her until she'd climbed inside and slammed the door shut, his senses feeling all kinds of crazy. He'd wanted to do that since the first time he'd laid eyes on her. Now he wished he hadn't.

Chapter Two

"We've got a bull down, Pop." Sean MacLaren stepped into Rafe's office, setting his cowboy hat upside down on the desk and dragging an arm across his forehead.

"Which one?" Rafe lifted his head from the paper he'd been reviewing, his brows drawing together.

"Ghost Rider. One of our best rodeo bulls down within forty-eight hours of loading him for the rodeo. Emilio had Fritz call the doc," Sean said, referring to their stock manager and his assistant.

Sean had known Fritz for years. They'd become casual friends, meeting for drinks with a group of buddies and playing together on a local baseball team. When it became apparent Emilio needed an assistant, he had no problem recommending Fritz for the job.

Sean grabbed a cup, placing it beneath the spout of the one-cup coffee maker and selecting the boldest choice in the assortment his father kept handy. When Rafe returned from his first trip to Fire Mountain in years, he'd surprised his sons by tossing out the old glass canister contraption he'd had forever, replacing it with one of those new single cup machines like his brothers owned. Sean had to admit, it made real fine coffee.

"Any of the others appear sick?" Rafe grabbed the

upcoming rodeo schedule, deciding which bull to send as a replacement for Ghost Rider. Last minute adjustments were common, but usually for reasons other than sickness of one of their top bulls.

"Not that Emilio or Fritz can tell. Fritz and the men are moving the rest of the stock to the other yard, cleaning up the pens, washing them down, and sanitizing the equipment." Sean sipped coffee while he stared out on the stockyards, knowing Fritz and Emilio would take care of whatever needed to be done. Every season brought new challenges such as increased cost of feed, sickness, or stiffer competition from new companies entering the rodeo stock contracting business. They'd weather this one as they did every obstacle. "When does Mitch return?"

"He drove in late last night. I expect he'll walk in any minute." Rafe grabbed the phone on the first ring. "MacLaren."

Sean waited until his father finished the call. He knew they still hadn't heard whether they'd gotten a big contract for a rodeo in the Midwest. They'd held the contract for years and until recently, no one could come close to the quality of stock, dependability, and prices. A competitor, Double Ace Bucking Stock, emerged over the last few years with deep pockets and staying power, pushing some of the old timers to the sidelines. They'd have a fight on their hands if they tried to dislodge RTC Bucking Bulls. Finally, Rafe set the phone down.

"Well?" Sean prompted.

"We got it, but according to my contact, not by much.

Double Ace undercut us. The factors in our favor included our past affiliation with them and excellent record. No promises going forward. I don't know how we'll keep it next year with the prices they're offering." Rafe pushed from the desk, joining his son at the window. "My contact said Double Ace hired a new rodeo committee director, someone who's grown up in the ranch business. He competed through school and into the pros until an injury knocked him out of the circuit. Kid's got deep ties in ranching and lots of chits to call in when needed."

"He give you a name?" Sean asked.

"Nope, and I didn't ask. Figured we could find out on our own." He spun around at the sound of the door opening.

"Sorry I'm late. Couldn't seem to pull myself out from under the covers." Mitch entered, shaking their hands. "Damn, I must be getting old. The miles seemed to stretch forever. Coffee?" He looked around, remembering the new machine and made a cup, enjoying the aroma. "Anything new on the contract?"

"We got it." Rafe explained what he'd learned.

"Guess we'd better find out who this new guy is and how they're able to undercut us by so much." Mitch knew the business had evolved, and once again, thanked the outcome of the merger with MacLaren Enterprises. He'd resented his uncles at first, not understanding their dogged desire to purchase RTC over the objections of Rafe. Now he understood. The clout of the combined companies provided important resources RTC needed to compete with new upstart organizations fat with money. The downside included having more eyes watching over your shoulder and second guessing decisions.

"We'll put Skye on it. She's out there every day talking to members of the rodeo committees and is privy to much of what's going on. I'm surprised she hasn't heard rumors about Double Ace's man and how he's getting his foot in the door." Rafe picked up the phone and dialed his oldest daughter. "Skye, it's Dad. Give me a call as soon as you get this."

"You glad to be back?" Sean took a seat across the desk from Rafe, watching Mitch stare at the corrals.

"Sure."

Sean glanced at his father, his eyes narrowing for a moment before he turned in the chair to face Mitch. "You don't sound too certain."

He shifted, pulling himself out of whatever gloom had plagued him since leaving Fire Mountain. "Of course I'm certain. Glad to leave all the drama with the relatives behind and get back to what I know. Now, where do you want me to start?"

******

Fire Mountain, Arizona

"What do you think?" Dana asked Eric as he studied the new marketing material for changing the RTC Bucking Bulls logo to a design more consistent with MacLaren

Enterprises.

"Have you shown this to anyone else?"

"You're the first as I want an unbiased view. Since you're in the real estate and development side of the business, not the bucking stock side, I thought you might have some insights before I present it to Amber, then Heath, Jace, and Rafe."

"I'm guessing Rafe will be the last to see it." Eric chuckled at the way people at headquarters still treated Rafe with a measure of uncertainty. With good reason. No one ever knew how he, or Mitch, would react to new ideas for RTC.

Rafe had been the brother to approach their father years ago about adding bulls to the existing saddle and bareback riding stock business. Clark MacLaren had turned him down without discussion, prompting a blow up that never resolved itself before the elder MacLaren died. It had been why Rafe left the family, not returning until years later when Heath and Jace made an offer to purchase RTC.

After establishing the bucking bull business with two friends, they penciled out how they'd operate and made few changes in all their years in business, other than expanding their breeding program. Rafe resisted change the same way his father had years before, and it appeared Mitch kept the same skeptical attitude.

"Rafe is a little difficult to convince of new ideas, but so is Mitch. It must run in that branch of the family." Dana pursed her lips, having no idea why she'd brought up his name. There'd been no reason for it. "Anyway, what do you think?"

Eric glanced up from where he studied the mock up alongside the existing RTC and MacLaren logos, choosing not to respond to her comment about Mitch. No one wanted to get in the middle of whatever fireworks always resulted when the two of them were together.

"Maybe tone down the background and shadow the image. Amber will no doubt have other suggestions. Is she your next stop?" He handed the draft back to her.

"In five minutes, then I'll take off to make the modifications." Dana picked up her briefcase, then slung her purse over her shoulder. "Have you heard anything from Mitch since he left? I mean…if he arrived home safe and all." He'd been gone for several days, and from what she knew, no one had heard a word. She tried to make her question sound casual while she killed time until Amber would be in her office. Amusement sparkling in Eric's eyes told her she hadn't succeeded.

"Nope. Not a word. I thought he might get in touch with you first." His mouth tilted up at the corners as he leaned back in his chair and laced his hands behind his head.

"Me? That's a laugh. I'm the last person he'd contact." Dana shifted on her feet, uncomfortable she'd brought him up.

"Not sure I believe that, but I'll let you know if I do hear from him." Eric didn't mention he and Amber had witnessed the way Dana and Mitch said goodbye when they'd left Heath's.

"No worries." She shrugged, wishing she'd kept her mouth shut. "Thanks for the suggestions."

Dana grabbed a bottle of water from the lounge, gulping a large amount before walking down the hall toward Amber's office. She continued to chastise herself for bringing up Mitch, not once but twice, as she joined her friend, set down her water and dropped into a chair.

Amber hung up from a call, watching Dana's face morph from exhaustion or confusion, she couldn't tell which, to a mask of determination. Over the last week she'd been acting in a way Amber had seen once before—when the man everyone thought she'd marry dropped the bomb on her that he'd met someone else. He'd made the declaration without emotion, as if he hadn't cared at all what his words had done to her heart. Even now, Amber didn't believe her friend had recovered, at least not enough to fall in love again.

"Are you all right?"

"A little tired from staying up late to work on this." Dana handed Amber the mockup of her logo idea.

"You sure that's all? You look, well, distant. Not quite all here."

Darn it, Dana thought, forgetting how well Amber could read her. They'd been friends since Amber first arrived in Denver, starting a job at the same company where Dana worked.

"No big deal. I've felt a little off for a few days. You know, as if my feet aren't quite planted as solid as I'd like.

23

I'll be fine, really."

"It wouldn't have anything to do with Mitch, would it?"

Dana huffed out a breath, straightening her spine. "Of course not. Why would I waste a moment thinking about someone as rude and surly as him?"

"No reason, except the lip lock you gave him before he left."

"Were you watching us?" Her indignant tone was mixed with stunned disbelief that anyone had witnessed something she was trying hard to forget.

"We weren't until Eric spotted you next to Mitch's truck when we walked out of the house. He, uh, pushed a button on his watch and started timing it."

"He didn't," Dana groaned, placing her face in her hands and shaking her head. "Why haven't you said anything before?"

"I figured you'd say something when you were ready. You were so quiet the last time we spoke, and you're the same today. Do you want to talk about it?"

"No. It wasn't what it seemed. Just a goodbye kiss, nothing more. Besides, I'm going out with Kell, remember?" Dana's expression didn't quite match the hard tone of her words.

"And how is that going?" Amber didn't believe for a minute the intense kiss she'd witnessed meant nothing.

"Fine. We've gotten together quite a bit, and no, we are not sleeping together."

Amber laughed, shaking her head. "No kissing,

anything?"

"I didn't say that. It's just we haven't gone to bed, although Kell would like it to move in that direction."

"And you? What do you want?" Amber knew how hard Dana worked to keep her emotions in check, never allowing another man to get under her skin.

Out of nowhere, the fight faded from Dana's eyes as she slumped back in the chair. "I don't know. Kell didn't kiss me until after I'd kissed Mitch. As much as I wanted to be blown away, it didn't happen. I never thought much about Mitch, except how to stay as far away from him as possible. But that kiss...I've never experienced anything like it."

"Didn't you say it was just a kiss?" Amber asked, her voice full of empathy.

"Yeah...about that." Dana glanced across the table at Amber. "I lied. It felt pretty amazing." She laughed, although there didn't seem to be much humor behind it.

"Wow."

"Yeah." Dana shook her head and edged closer to the front of the chair, taking a deep breath. "You and I both know he's *not* the man for me and I am absolutely *not* the woman he needs. Besides, he's gone."

"And Kell is here," Amber reminded her.

"Right...and there's nothing wrong with him at all. So, what do you think of the logo?" Dana asked, changing the subject.

"I like it. You may want to tone down the background, shadow the RTC image a little." Amber snapped her head up at Dana's laugh. "What?"

"Nothing, except that's exactly what your husband said."

"Ah." She grinned. "Great minds and all that. Anything else you want me to see?"

"Nothing else. I'll make the changes for the meeting with Heath and Jace tomorrow. Will you be there?"

"Of course." As the head of marketing, Amber sat in on any subject touching on the presentation of their properties or products.

Dana picked up her purse and turned toward the door.

"Dana?"

"Yeah?"

"Forget about the kiss."

"I will." *Someday*, she thought as she headed toward the parking lot.

******

Crooked Tree

"I can't believe you're considering putting the house up for sale." Mitch's tone left no doubt how he felt about Rafe selling the seven bedroom home with eight baths, along with the guesthouse in back. Rafe and Mitch's mother had built the house while she was pregnant with Skye. The three youngest had never known another home, and to Mitch and Sean, it stood as a symbol of their heritage.

"Samantha's at the University of Montana and Rhett graduates from high school next year. He plans to follow Sam to Missoula. This place is too big for just me." Rafe handed Mitch a glass of water. He had hoped to keep the possible sale a secret, but his real estate agent left a few minutes after Mitch arrived. "Besides, I'd sell the ranch and guest house, then build another, smaller home on the other end of the property. We'd lose a few acres, but retain about four hundred." He and his ex-wife, Deirdre, planned the location of the house on one corner of the property, figuring one day they'd want a smaller place.

"Does Mom know you're thinking of selling?"

"I gave her cash when the divorce went through, so no, she doesn't. And it's none of her business."

She'd relocated to southern California to join her longtime lover who had a home on the water, as well as a large log home near Big Sky, Montana, where'd they'd met. The four youngest had been rocked by the news their mother had been involved in an affair. Mitch hadn't been surprised. He'd learned of the deceit years before, keeping it quiet until he felt honor-bound to make sure Rafe knew about it.

"Have you signed the papers for a listing?"

"Not yet, why?" Rafe settled into one of the large leather chairs in the great room.

"Maybe I could figure a way to buy it." Mitch didn't know what triggered the offer except nostalgia, and he had no idea how he'd ever pay for it.

Rafe studied him, knowing Mitch also hated change. However, Rafe hadn't thought selling the house would have such an impact on him.

"I'm just considering a sale at this point. It's paid off, so there's no rush."

"All right. But you'll let me know if you decide to sell, right? You'd better not try to sell it out from under me." Mitch drained the glass of water, setting it on the counter.

"I'll let you know," Rafe replied. "Are you going to tell me what's had you so tied up in your office over the last few days?"

"It's not much. I'm penciling out some ideas I've been nurturing for a while. Unless I think there's promise, you might not hear about any of them."

"Heath and Jace want me to work down at headquarters with them."

"Yeah, I know. It's not for a while though, right?" Mitch asked.

"Sooner than I first thought. You think you're ready to take over the reins of the company if I leave in a month?"

"A month? That's a lot sooner than I thought."

"I spoke with Heath yesterday," Rafe said. "We're in the discussion stage at this point, nothing definite. What do you think?"

Mitch had dreamed of this chance since making the decision to follow his father in the business while in high school. Rafe had insisted he finish college, working summers in the company. He'd done some bull riding while in school, despite knowing his dreams of following his father at RTC would preclude a professional rodeo career. The lessons he'd learned competing stuck with him, as well as the contacts, and he'd put it all to good use.

Rafe's partners, Chris and Ty, had finished their obligation of continuing with the business a few months after the sale. Everyone knew Mitch, Sean, and Skye were being groomed to take over their responsibilities, allowing Chris and Ty to pursue other ventures. The three men had been friends since high school, but Rafe had always been the driving force behind RTC.

"What do you think?" Mitch's question held a hint of uncertainty.

"Hell, son, you know I think you're ready. This one's on you. If you don't have the confidence—"

"I'm ready."

Rafe barked out a laugh. "Of course you are. The question is, am I?"

"What are you saying?"

"This may not be a short-term position. I may take over a whole new division in the company, meaning I may not be back for quite a spell."

Mitch expected it would be a few months, maybe a year, then the position would revert back to his father.

"Is that the real reason you're thinking about selling the house?"

"I've been thinking on it for some time. You kids have your own lives. Maybe it's my turn to take on new responsibilities, travel a bit—"

"Get to know Kade?" Mitch's relationship with his

half-brother had improved during his stint in Fire Mountain, to the point he enjoyed spending time with him, even if they might never became tight friends.

Rafe's gaze focused on Mitch, who'd been the oldest until Kade reappeared in their lives. Mitch had been angry, Kade had been indifferent, wanting nothing from his father or siblings, people he never knew existed until a year before.

"That's part of it, too. It's my fault he grew up without a father or the opportunities you and the others were given. He's done well, seems to have no regrets. I'm the one with the guilt."

Mitch stood, pacing to the bar and picking up a bottle of Crown. He poured two shots, handing one to Rafe.

"I know this isn't a popular opinion, but it seems to me it's his mother who's the guilty party."

Rafe studied the dark amber liquid, swishing it in the glass before taking a sip. "I suppose there's lots of blame to go around and no answers. Reyna should've told me, yes, but I understand her reasons for keeping Kade from me. Regardless, it's my chance to get to know him." He finished his drink then checked the time. "It's Friday night. Shouldn't you be out with friends or on a date?"

"I'm meeting some buddies in a while. Guess I'd better get ready."

"Glad you're back." Rafe tipped his empty glass toward Mitch.

"Same here."

Chapter Three

Fire Mountain

"Buying this has to be the best decision I've ever made." Dana pulled off her helmet, swinging her right leg off the seat as she scanned her new motorcycle. The black and chrome finish with red trim seemed a little tame, yet in her mind, the Harley had it all. She couldn't wait to take it on a long ride, maybe even a few days if she could get the time off.

Amber had called earlier, asking if she wanted to go for ride with her, Eric, Brooke, and Kade. She'd jumped at the chance to try out her new bike with the others along. Amber broke down and purchased a new bike shortly after the wedding, but also liked to ride on the back seat of Eric's bagger.

"You sure handle it well." Brooke climbed off the back seat of Kade's bike, admiring Dana's new purchase.

"Why don't you get one?" Dana asked between large swallows of water.

"Oh, no. I'm quite happy holding on to Kade as he maneuvers this beast. Besides, Jace selected a new horse for me so Cassie can teach me barrel racing." Brooke's smile lit her face. She'd talked about learning the sport ever since she and Kade married.

"Cassie and I've spoken about her teaching me also.

I'd love to join you." Dana slid the empty bottle into a saddlebag and secured the strap.

"That's going to be a little hard with her moving to Cold Creek, Colorado to work with Cam," Eric said, surprised neither his sister nor Dana had heard about Cassie's promotion.

"What, she's moving? Cassie never mentioned it." Dana's smile vanished at the news. They'd become close friends, hanging out in the evenings and riding their horses on the weekends.

"Heath told her yesterday. She'll start by working with the rodeo committees, working on proposals to supply saddle and bareback stock, plus whatever else is required. Cassie is smart and a quick learner, but it will demand almost all her time. It includes traveling more than she's been doing here." Eric handed Amber a sandwich as everyone found seats around a picnic table in the state campground. It had become a favorite stop on their weekend rides.

"I'm glad you asked me along. This is beautiful." Dana bit into her sandwich, washing it down with a diet soda as she watched ducks swim in circles around the lake.

"You're welcome to come anytime. Mitch used to join us before he took off north." Kade turned on the bench so his legs stretched out in front of him and crossed his ankles. "I'll bet he's going to miss these rides when he's shoveling out of a couple feet of snow next winter."

"Maybe, but I'm guessing not enough to get him back down here." Eric tossed his empty wrapper into a trash bin and stood, stretching his arms above his head.

"I don't believe Mitch hates it here as much as he wanted us to believe. It's just his way, that's all." Kade held out a hand to Brooke. "You ready to roll?" He nodded toward the bike.

Dana listened to the banter about Mitch, trying to suppress her curiosity. For once she didn't ask questions, hoping to learn something about the man she couldn't stop thinking about. The kiss stayed with her for days after he'd left, and even now, she could almost feel his mouth touching hers, taste the mixture of coffee and peppermint on his lips. An involuntary shudder coursed through her at the memory. She wished they'd either had more time to explore the earth-shattering contact or that it had never happened.

"I'll bet you're glad he's gone and not ragging on you all the time." Amber slid on her helmet, watching Dana do the same.

Dana shrugged, tightening the chin strap. "His barbs never bothered me. Mitch is a brooding 'ole cuss who isn't happy unless he finds fault with something. I made an easy target."

"You think?"

Dana laughed at Amber's unexpected sarcasm. "Yeah, guess I walked into a lot of his gibes. He's so different from most of you—except Rafe, of course. It's easy to see they're related."

Eric walked up, catching Dana's last comment. "Heath mentioned Rafe may be moving down here, working with him and Jace on a new business venture. It's expected Mitch will take over for him as president of RTC if that happens."

"What new venture? I haven't heard anything about it." Brooke asked as she and Kade stopped next to the others. As part of the senior staff, they would normally bring her in early when discussing a new venture.

"I'm not privy to the information either. I happened to walk into Heath's office when he, Jace, and Rafe were finishing a call. Caught bits and pieces, but it sounded like a done deal." Eric grabbed his keys and swung a leg over his bike. "You all ready to ride?"

******

Dana sat outside Heath's office, waiting for him to finish another meeting before seeing her. He'd called her early, wanting to meet before he took off with Annie for a few days at the family cabin a few hours away. The place had a lake view, running water, electricity, no phone, and no Internet—everything Heath needed to relax.

"Sorry about the wait. Come on in." Heath stepped aside, letting Dana walk past him. "Do you want some coffee, water?"

"Nothing for me, thanks." She glanced around, then took a seat, surprised neither Amber nor Eric were included. As an outside contractor, she always attended meetings with one of the two when she presented her work to Heath or Jace, and more recently, Rafe.

"You know, of course, with Rafe arriving in Fire Mountain, Mitch has been promoted to president of RTC." Heath paced toward the window, looking out on the expansive view—all of it MacLaren land.

"Yes, I heard about it from Amber and Eric."

"Rafe will be taking the lead on a new business venture, which we'll be announcing in a few weeks, along with some other changes. The changes are why I asked to meet with you."

Dana's stomach churned. The work from MacLaren Enterprises kept her afloat, allowing her to have a measure of freedom instead of living from hand to mouth. Losing this job would mean a long search for other work to replace the lost income. She took a deep breath.

"I see."

"We're rolling out a few changes early, before announcing the remaining actions to the entire company." He took a seat across from her, leaning forward. "We're growing, which means we need expanded services and prefer to utilize our own employees."

Dana caught her lower lip between her teeth, waiting. She did not want to hear the rest, assuming they'd already found someone with more experience who could add more value to the company.

"Amber tells me you have a degree in marketing with an additional major in graphic design. Is that right?"

"It is. I didn't realize how much I enjoyed the design part until I took an elective course. The professor thought I had talent, so he encouraged me to continue."

"Have you had any experience in general marketing?" Heath's expression showed no hint of his thoughts.

"For the first two years I worked as a marketing rep, then as a marketing manager. When a position came up in the design department, I jumped on it. The truth is I enjoy all of it. I did try to move back into a marketing manager role, but never made it before my position was cut in the last set of layoffs." Dana's eyes sharpened on Heath, trying to assess his question.

"We—Jace, Rafe, and I—have a proposition for you. Amber needs help in marketing and has requested we hire a marketing manager to work with the stock contracting companies. The job would include graphic design and reports to Amber. Are you interested?"

Dana couldn't contain the smile which spread across her face. "Yes, of course. I'm very interested."

"Good." He slid a folder across the desk to her. "Here's the offer, benefit package, and all the details of the job. Read through it. I'd appreciate your answer by the first of next week."

She gripped the edge of the folder, dying to tear into it, but deciding the professional approach would be to thank Heath and graciously leave. Then scream with excitement in the parking lot.

"Thank you, Heath. I'll get back to you right away."

"Get in touch with Jace if you have any questions while I'm gone."

"I will. And again, thank you."

******

Crooked Tree

"Moonshine and two other bulls are down, Mitch. The same symptoms as Ghost Rider. Emilio's already called the doc, and he has Fritz and the men going through the same process they did before—moving the stock, changing the feed, sanitizing everything." Sean sat down, pinching the bridge of his nose. "What do you think is going on?"

"Hell if I know. The investigation showed tainted feed from a supplier we've used for over ten years. The company checked all their customers plus delivered and stored feed. No other sick animals, and all their feed tested clean. Ghost Rider is finally able to compete, and now Moonshine and the others are down. I'd better get back in touch with the supplier."

"Someone's getting access to the cattle, Mitch. I'm certain of it."

Mitch set the phone down without dialing. "What are you saying?"

"Think about it. Several bulls getting sick within a short time of each other and the symptoms appear the same."

Mitch leaned back in his chair, rubbing knuckles across his chin. "Let's wait to hear what the doc says before thinking along those lines. The bulls could have come down with something different than Ghost Rider."

"Maybe, but my gut is gnawing at me and that's never a good sign."

The phone rang three times before Mitch reached for it, holding up a hand for Sean to stay.

"Mitch, it's Skye."

"Where have you been? I expected to hear from you yesterday."

"It's good to hear from you, too, big brother. And yes, I'm fine, having a wonderful time in the beautiful Midwest. And how are things with you?"

"Knock it off, Skye. Give me some good news."

"What's going on?"

"Sean's in my office. Moonshine and two other bulls came down sick."

"The same as Ghost Rider?"

"We don't know yet. Doc's on her way. So, what have you learned?"

Skye held the phone between her ear and shoulder, juggling a soda as she pulled open her notes. "There isn't as much as I'd hoped. My rodeo committee contacts aren't talking other than vague information about Double Ace."

"Tell me what you know. I'm putting you on speaker so Sean can hear."

They heard a drawn out slurping sound, then the sounds of shuffling before Skye's voice came through.

"Hey, Sean."

"Skye. Tell us what you found out."

"Double Ace is owned by a group out of Mexico and a couple of U.S. citizens. Big money and lots of layers. I haven't been able to get names of owners or contacts. It's all pretty strange as people who'd normally spill what they know aren't talking. I did learn there are two men who represent the company to the committees across the country. Both ex-rodeo and well-known. One has been with Double Ace since they started. The other just came on a few months ago and is my main competition."

"You got his name?" Sean asked.

"Garner. Matt Garner. Either of you know him?"

Sean looked at Mitch, who wore a blank expression

"Nope. Have you met him?" Mitch asked Skye.

"Not yet. At some point I'm sure we'll connect. I did learn some committees are wary of them, but they have an obligation to take a serious look at their proposals because of the bottom line."

"Did you get any firm numbers? How much less than us they're coming in?" Sean leaned in closer to the speaker as the line began to cut in and out.

"No one's talking percentages or dollars."

"All right. We know they have deep pockets, two rodeo committee contacts—one named Matt Garner." Mitch scratched on a legal pad as he spoke, shaking his head, then tossing the pen aside. "Not much."

"I know. I'll get more, it takes time. Has anyone heard from Pop?"

"Sean and I have a conference call with him every morning at seven o'clock. He sounds good. When will you be back?" Mitch continued to stare at the information on Double Ace. Nothing indicated how they operated or their pricing.

"End of the week."

"She's got a hot date," Sean joked, smiling at Mitch.

"My dates are none of your business. Besides, he's a nice guy. Well, I've got to run. I'll call as soon as I learn more."

******

Fire Mountain

"Have you made a decision?" Amber sat on the floor in Dana's living room, resting her back against the sofa, sipping a glass of wine while sharing Chinese takeout.

"I'd be a fool if I didn't take the offer, and you know it." Dana dipped an egg roll in plum sauce then hot mustard before taking a bite. "This was your idea, right?"

"Yes and no. Heath came to me a few weeks ago about some vague plans to expand. I didn't get any details, enough to get a picture of what he, Jace, and Rafe have planned and the expected revenue. He asked if I could continue as a one person department or would need help. I told him it would be difficult alone, but I could do it if needed. I mentioned your name as a suggestion. The next I knew he called me into a meeting with the brothers where they told me about their plans to make you an offer. So, I'm guessing your answer is yes."

Dana's broad smile held the answer. "I left a message with Jace tonight." She topped off Amber's glass, then her own.

"And the part about supporting the stock contracting

companies?"

Her face lost none of its glow at the reminder. "It doesn't matter to me which groups I work with, one is the same as another. Cam and I get along well, and I can handle Mitch."

"If you say so."

"I'm guessing it was your idea how to split up the work, so why are you so worried about it?" Dana grabbed another egg roll, taking a large bite.

"Actually, Heath made the decision. He felt it would be an easier transition since both companies deal with the same rodeos and prepare joint proposals. Their marketing needs are similar, even if they operate separately."

"For now. I imagine at some point they'll end up being combined into one group. I hear Cassie loves Cold Creek."

"She likes anything that's a challenge. Guess I'd better pick up Eric. He went over to Kade's to watch a baseball game. Brooke's out of town, so there's no telling what trouble the two will get themselves into."

"Heck, he could walk home if needed." Heath and Jace built a series of cabins several years before, all furnished with two bedrooms, one bath, and a complete kitchen. Brooke and Kade lived in one, Eric and Amber in another, with Cam and Lainey using one when they came to Fire Mountain. Until he'd left, Mitch occupied a fourth cabin.

"True, he could and probably should. When do you start the new job?"

"I'll be knocking on your door bright and early

Monday morning." She gave Amber a hug, waiting to go inside until Amber had slid inside Eric's truck and started the engine.

Turning her back to the door, she leaned against it, thinking again of her new position. She'd given notice at her regular job as a part-time instructor at the community college. With no classes over the summer, the timing worked in her favor. Her other contract client needed her three to four hours a week, which she hoped to still handle with her new job.

Dana picked up the empty glasses and shoved the cork back into the almost empty bottle of wine. The excitement at the new opportunity both exhilarated and frightened her. She had no doubt about her abilities to work with Cam and Cassie. Mitch would be a challenge, yet one she welcomed. He would test her patience, yet as long as she kept her distance, stayed professional and remote, she had no doubt they'd work well together.

Yep, no doubt at all.

Chapter Four

Crooked Tree

"Long time no see, Mitch. Where have you been keeping yourself?"

Mitch glanced up from daydreaming into his beer to see Lizzie, a curvy, dark-haired beauty he'd shared numerous nights with over the years. He hadn't seen her in a while—since about the time his father had dropped the news about Kade on the family. Turning from his spot at the bar, he rested his back and arms against it. Starting at her five-inch high heels, he let his gaze wander up her long, lean legs to her rounded hips and slim waist, then to what had first drawn his attention to her years before. His mouth quirked up at the memory as his eyes focused on hers.

"Lizzie."

She looked around, not seeing a second drink, purse, or any indication he came with someone.

"Buy a girl a drink?" She settled onto a stool next to him, then turned, a smug smile on her face.

He turned back toward the bar, motioning to the bartender. "A Manhattan for the lady."

She touched his arm, letting a finger trail up to his shoulder before dropping it to grasp the conical-shaped glass holding the deep red cocktail. "Are you going to tell me where you've been hiding? It's been much too long."

Mitch watched as she took a sip, dragging her tongue across her lips, soaking up every delicious taste of whiskey, sweet vermouth, bitters, and cherry juice. His body tightened at the suggestive movements, knowing Lizzie did nothing without a purpose. Her intentions tonight held no mystery.

"I've been working out of town. Got back about a month ago."

"And you haven't called. Should I be insulted?"

"No insult. I've been busy." He sipped his beer, deciding whether or not to take Lizzie up on her obvious offer of an evening together. "What about you? Any changes?"

She waved her hand back and forth as if her answer was unimportant. "Same 'ole stuff. Work and play." Taking another sip of her Manhattan, she looked him over, then let her mouth curve into a seductive grin. "No one special in my life. And you?"

A bitter laugh escaped as he leaned forward, resting his arms on the bar. "I've got a lot of special people in my life. None I want to take to bed."

As soon as the words were out, an image of Dana popped into his head—her red hair framing a face sprinkled with freckles and the brightest, bluest eyes he'd ever seen. She laughed at him or with him, he could never tell which. Mitch shook his head to clear it of the image. The one woman whose presence could set him on edge had to be the same woman who plagued his dreams. He blamed himself and his impulsive dare for her to kiss him goodbye.

Expecting Dana to turn him down flat, he'd been stunned when she'd reached up to place a kiss on his cheek. His taunt backfired when the touch of her lips set off an explosion of senses beyond anything he'd ever experienced. Pulling her close, kissing her until both lacked breath had been stupid, and still played with his head. He'd woken up more than one night, sheets soaked, with images of Dana, moist lips and glazed eyes, racing through his head. He had to get her out of there.

Before he could change his mind, Mitch finished his drink, nodded for her to do the same, then grabbed her hand. "Let's get out of here."

******

Fire Mountain

"Where is Kell taking you tonight?" Amber sat on the edge of Dana's bed, watching her brush her hair then apply lip gloss.

"He didn't say. Some place casual, which is never a problem for me." She set the brush down, catching her lower lip between her teeth. "We always have a great time no matter what he plans. It's just..."

"It's just what?"

"He has everything I'd ever want, yet there's something missing. I wish I knew what."

45

"Maybe you need to give it time. It's only been a few weeks."

"True, and we see each other once, sometimes twice a week, and we're often with others." Dana stood, smoothed her top down over her tight jeans, and grabbed her purse. "Don't pay any attention to me. I'm just being an idiot."

Amber walked into the living room as someone knocked at the door. "Hey, Kell. Come on in, she's almost ready."

"I am ready." Dana came out of the bedroom as if she had no doubts at all about the man a few feet away, watching her as if he couldn't wait to get her alone. "Don't you look nice," she said. And he did—tight jeans, charcoal gray t-shirt stretched over well-honed muscles, and hair a little messy from the wind. "Where are we going?"

"I better take off. Good to see you, Kell." Amber disappeared outside.

Kell took a few steps forward, stopping within a foot of Dana, and slid his hands down her arms, feeling the slight tremble.

"It's a beautiful Saturday. I thought we could go to the batting cage, then stop at a new antique store in town before dinner. Sound good?" He grasped her hands, thumbs rubbing slow circles on her palms, his steel-gray eyes boring into hers.

Dana swayed at his touch and the sight of magnetic eyes turning a dark smoke color.

As if receiving a slap on the back of her head, Dana decided to let her inhibitions go and do what her body had been demanding for weeks—assuming he still wanted the same. From the look in his eyes and his closeness, she assumed he did. Clearing her throat, she stepped back, plastering a haughty smile on her face.

"Sounds great."

"Afterwards, perhaps I can persuade you to come back here for coffee or a drink or..."

Kell's eyes crinkled at the corners as he shot her a devastating grin. "I think I might be persuaded."

The afternoon couldn't have gone better. She loved practicing at the batting cage, taking all her stress out on those balls coming toward her at sixty miles per hour. They rotated, each taking a break while the other batted. Kell kept his speed at seventy, a good speed for someone who'd played high school and college ball but had been away from the game for years.

"How come you didn't try out for the pros?" Dana asked as she replaced him in the batter's box.

"Who says I didn't?"

Dana stopped, letting the bat rest at her side. "Really? You tried out?"

He chuckled, although his eyes remained serious. "I did. Other life events got in the way and it seemed more appropriate to go straight into law school. I'd always planned to be a lawyer, and besides, I knew my talents weren't quite strong enough for a major league career. It was a good decision."

She stared at him a moment longer before taking her spot in the box and swinging at the oncoming balls, reminding herself to ask him more about those life-changing events.

The new antique store Kell took her to turned out to be a refurbished warehouse loaded with merchandise from over forty vendors. Furniture, glassware, artwork, and all kinds of memorabilia adorned the space which spanned three levels.

"Look at this." Dana picked up a lamp from the early nineteen hundreds. "I swear my grandmother had one just like this. A pair of them, actually." She turned it over, noting the four hundred dollar price. "I wonder if they negotiate," she snorted before putting it down.

"My guess is everything in here is negotiable. We can talk to the woman at the front counter if you want, see what can be done."

"Nah. With the motorcycle payment and my horse, I can't fit one more item in my budget. It's nice to look, though. What do you have there?" She nodded toward a doll he had dangling from one hand.

"Nothing special. A doll I thought my daughter might like."

Dana's eyes grew wide. "You have a daughter? How come you've never mentioned her?"

He shrugged, picking up a book on one of the displays and thumbing through it. "It never came up. If you're done, I'll pay for this and explain it all over dinner."

They walked to an Italian restaurant a few doors down where he'd taken her before. It happened to be one of her favorites, where they served her enough to take home for leftovers. She vacillated between the pesto on angel hair pasta and the lasagna with sausage, finally settling on the lasagna. Kell's grin told her he'd decided on his usual *osso buco*.

She grabbed a piece of bruschetta, nibbling on it while she waited. After a few minutes of casual talk, she finished the bread and leaned forward.

"Tell me about your daughter."

Kell took a sip of wine, staring at the red liquid a few moments.

"Emma. She's four. That's why I moved to Fire Mountain. Her mother and I divorced a couple years ago, and she followed her boyfriend here. I didn't want to miss seeing Emma grow up. The prosecutor position became available at the perfect time, so I jumped on it."

They remained silent as the waiter set down their meals, each taking a few bites before Dana spoke.

"When were you planning to tell me about Emma?"

"Tonight. When you mentioned going back to your place, I realized you needed to know before our relationship went any further. Nothing in the world matters to me more than Emma. Maybe I'll remarry someday, maybe not, but Emma will always be a huge part of whatever I do."

She took another bite, chewing slowly. Dana loved children, always had, and hoped to have a few of her own, as in more than two. Right now, with her new job and the need to travel almost every week, the timing couldn't be worse.

"By the look on your face I can see this is a game changer for us." Kell sat back, crossing his arms. The last two years had been rough with the divorce, custody issues, and leaving a job he loved in the valley to follow his ex to Fire Mountain. Then he'd met Dana. Her uninhibited, frank manner captivated him from the first time he saw her. He still didn't know if it would turn in to love, at least the kind that would last, but he wanted the chance to find out.

"It's not about Emma. I like kids and want some of my own someday."

"Just not someone else's." He reached out and grabbed his glass of wine, swallowing what remained.

"I didn't say that, Kell. And honestly, I believe I'd have no issue being a stepmother. It's just...well, right now, the timing couldn't be worse. My new job requires travel to Montana and Colorado, and I just learned yesterday I may be supporting another group located in Texas. Heath's already broadening the scope of marketing work and I'm running as fast as possible to keep up."

"There's no denying it's a great opportunity for you." He split the remaining wine between her glass and his. "You know, it doesn't have to be all or nothing. You like kids, I like having you around. We could stop seeing each other, or we can continue as friends. Maybe you could join Emma and me once in a while, and the two of us could still meet for lunch or dinner, or—"

"Hit baseballs, go on hikes, rock climb." Dana smiled, thinking it a terrific idea, even if it did mean tucking her lust away for another time, and perhaps a different man.

He reached across the table, taking her hand in his. "Good. I like you too much to think about never seeing you again." Letting go, he sat back, and smiled. "Besides, I want to learn what happens to Dana Ballard and her adventures at Maclaren Enterprises."

******

"What do you think? Can we handle all of it?" Amber asked Dana as they reviewed the new structure of the marketing department presented to them at a management meeting earlier that morning.

"It's what you've wanted since you started." Dana continued to read through and highlight the increased responsibilities impacting her. "We'll be handling social media, website design, advertising, public relations, and be part of the acquisition team." She glanced up at Amber. "It's a lot for two people."

"Heath did give us a choice. Hire a third person or leave it a two person department, take on the additional work and divide the proposed salary between us. If we take on the work, and do it well, there's no telling when we'd have the chance to hire a new person. At least we'd get paid well for our efforts."

"Did he give you a number?"

Amber slid his memo across the desk, watching Dana almost choke on the water she'd just swallowed.

"That much?" Dana took the paper in her hand and

studied it.

"Split sixty to me and forty to you. If that's agreeable."

"Are you kidding?" She calculated her total pay with the increase. "It would take me a long time to get to this level. I say we take it on and bring in a new person when we are too exhausted to continue the load."

"Great. I'll let Heath know. Why don't each of us jot down ideas and meet about five o'clock today. I know you're heading out to visit Cam and Cassie, then up to Montana next week. Our strategy should be in place prior to you leaving."

"I'll meet you here at five."

"Dana?"

"Yeah?"

"Is everything all right with you and Kell?"

Dana hadn't mentioned a word about him since their date on Saturday, and it didn't take a genius to see something bothered her.

"Kell's divorced and has a daughter. He told me Saturday night at dinner."

"That's surprising. I would've thought he'd find that detail important enough to bring up before now. What are you going to do?"

"I understand why he waited, and I'm not angry about it. Her name's Emma and she's four." She smiled, remembering the look on Kell's face when he mentioned his daughter. "He's crazy about her. Anyway, we agreed to continue our friendship, but nothing more—at least for now."

"And you're okay with that?"

"Relieved, actually. I like Kell a lot and was prepared to heat things up. The news made me step back and take a look at my life. With the new job and added responsibilities, it would've been hard to find time for a relationship with him. Now there's no pressure. I'd like to meet Emma, spend time with them, but I don't want there to be issues if it never goes beyond a friendship."

"I understand. Having a county prosecutor on your bad side wouldn't be wise—for any of us," Amber joked, knowing Dana would understand her warped sense of humor.

"How true that is. After what happened to us a few months ago...well...I guess you never know how life will go. See you later this afternoon." Dana felt better having told someone about her and Kell. The changes at work meant all her concentration had to be focused somewhere else, and not on Kell or any other man.

Chapter Five

Crooked Tree

"The stock's loaded and ready to go, Mitch. Do you want to come out and check on it?" Sean stood halfway inside the door leading to a deck with stairs down to the stock pens.

"Don't see why I need to."

"You know how Pop was before he left for Arizona. Nothing ever happened without his oversight."

"Control. Yeah, I remember."

"It's a new driver and I thought you might want to meet her." Sean pushed his hat up on his head and smiled.

"Her? When did we start hiring women as drivers?" Mitch stood, grabbing his hat as he followed Sean outside, spotting the bright red cab right away. A compact female stood by the door, her eyes trained on them.

"Jeanie Naylor, this is my brother, Mitch, our president."

She stuck out her hand, a smile breaking the deep creases in her face from years in the sun. Her brown ponytail held streaks of gray, but her eyes sparkled as if she were a young girl.

"Mr. MacLaren. It's a pleasure."

"Nice to meet you, and call me Mitch." He didn't return her smile, glancing around her to check out the truck and the name on the door—Naylor Trucking. "When did you start driving for us?"

"This will be our first run for RTC. Is there a problem?"

"No problem, Jeanie. Mitch is always a little cautious about using a new crew, right?" He looked at Mitch, his eyes narrowing.

Mitch ignored Sean, choosing to walk the length of the truck.

"Can I answer any questions for you, Mitch?" Jeanie asked. She'd grown up in a man's world as the oldest of three daughters to an ex rodeo rider turned stock transporter. The sisters had ridden with him since they were old enough to walk, then during school breaks, learning to drive and expanding the business. He retired a few years before, leaving the business to his daughters.

"Who hired you?"

"Rafe met with me and my two sisters a few months ago. He said there'd been some problems with your former company, and he'd like to give us a shot. I got a call a few weeks ago to show up today."

Mitch blinked several times at the news his father had hired a group of women to take care of their valuable stock. He placed his hands on his hips and stared down at her.

"You certain it was Rafe MacLaren?"

"Of course I'm certain. It took me years of convincing to get a shot at this. You think I'd waste my gas, busting my balls to get here if it weren't a done deal?"

His eyes softened at her selection of words, a grin turning up the corners of his mouth. "Balls, huh?"

"Both men and women gotta have them in this business, young man. Now, do I drive out of here or unload the stock?"

He ignored her question as he walked toward Sean, talking in low tones before turning toward the office.

"What's it going to be, Sean?"

"You're good to take off."

"Fine. I don't want to end up unloading these bulls at midnight."

"Don't take it personally, Jeanie. Like I said, he's cautious. Keep me posted on your progress."

"No problem. And don't worry about the bulls. They will make it to Kansas City." Jeanie climbed into her already running rig and settled into her seat.

Sean didn't leave until she'd pulled onto the street and turned toward the interstate. He'd been as surprised as Mitch at their father's selection of Naylor Trucking. Rafe had always been a good 'ole boy, favoring men over women, except when it came to his daughters, Skye and Samantha. He took the steps two at a time, entering Mitch's office without knocking.

"What the hell was that about?"

Mitch hung up from his call and studied his brother. They got along well, even though two men couldn't be more different in temperament. Trusting and friendly, Sean accepted people for what they were or until they lost his trust in some way. His ability to turn an acquaintance into a friend eluded Mitch, who could count his close friends on a couple digits. And one sat across from him right now.

"You came in to ask me if I wanted to check out the new company. That's what I did, nothing more. Did you know Pop hired her?"

"He mentioned it. I figured you already knew." He snatched a cookie from the plate near the coffee. "You make these?" he smirked, already knowing Mitch hadn't.

"Lizzie dropped them off."

Sean almost missed the mumbled response, then burst out in laughter. "You're back with her? Thought that ended long ago."

"It's none of your damn business, but nothing ever started. We hook up when it's right for both of us. That's it. Period." He grabbed a folder and flipped it open. "Where's Skye? I thought she'd be in by now."

Sean checked his phone, reading a recent text message. "She's on her way in now. You may want to give her a break. Between the truck breaking down and losing the contract in Arkansas, she's not in the best of moods."

"Excuses don't help us win business," Mitch groused as the door burst open.

"Hi, big brothers. Seems like forever since I've seen you." She gave each a hug then took a seat next to Sean.

"Coffee?" Sean asked.

"Love some. Did Naylor Trucking pick up the stock this morning?"

Sean glanced at Mitch before answering. "Jeanie left

not thirty minutes ago. It was the first time she and Mitch met."

"Ah..." Skye said before pursing her lips in a thin line.

"What's that supposed to mean?" Mitch glared at Skye then Sean, irritated at the silent language flowing between them.

"Just that you probably didn't know Naylor is now run by the sisters, not their dad. It's no secret you can still be a chauvinist when it comes to women in what some consider a man's job. Although I don't know how you can be with me and Sam as your sisters."

"You and Samantha grew up around stock animals and the rodeo. Besides you are dealing with rodeo committees. Lots of women and men in that job."

"But thirty years ago there weren't. A lot fewer women drove big rigs or were big animal vets like Gayle Wheaton. Or rode bikes like your Harley. Now a ton of women own bikes and handle them as well or better than men." She took the cup Sean handed her, then looked across the desk at Mitch. "All I'm saying is women are working in a lot of jobs that only men held when you were born. Times change."

The mere mention of a woman on a Harley hijacked Mitch's thoughts, allowing an image of Dana, with hair flying from under her helmet, to capture his mind. His body responded the same as it had each time he saw her on her bike. Shifting in his chair, he tried to get comfortable before his unease became apparent to Sean and Skye. He'd heard from Kade she'd purchased a bigger bike and had been riding with them. Not for the first time he thought about all he missed in Fire Mountain by returning to Crooked Tree, but he'd long ago accepted his responsibility to the family business. Besides, the work seemed to be the one stable part of his life.

"Well, let them change. I can be as flexible as the next man as long as there's a reason for it."

"Yeah, right," Skye snorted, drinking the steaming liquid and rolling her eyes.

"Enough of this. Did you learn any more about Double Ace's rodeo man, Matt Garner?" Mitch glanced at his notes from their call the week before.

"Not much. He rode in the PBR a few seasons before getting injured. Made good money and improved each year. Bets were he would've finished in the top group at the National Finals the year he took his last fall. From what I learned, he's considered one of the good guys. Oh, and he grew up somewhere in Arizona."

That got Mitch's attention. "You hear where?"

"Nope. It's a big state and they have contenders from all parts. I'll keep digging, maybe call Pop and have him run the name by Heath and Jace." She grabbed a cookie from the plate and took a bite. "Wow, this is great. You make these?"

Mitch groaned, rubbing his eyes with the palms of his hands as Sean burst into laughter.

******

59

"Thanks for calling me about the ride. I hoped to get out one more time before the trip." Dana strapped on her helmet and swung her leg over the seat, then watched as the others did the same. She, Cassie, Brooke, and Amber rode their horses at least twice a week after work and on Sundays, reserving Saturdays for motorcycle rides.

"Everyone ready?" Kade called, then powered his Harley toward the main highway with Brooke holding on from the back seat. Dana rode hers behind Kade, and Eric and Amber followed her on their bikes.

Today they'd ride to one of the lakes an hour east of Fire Mountain. Dana fell into a rhythm of watching the traffic, then glancing at the passing scenery. Before he left, she rode behind Mitch, following his moves and admiring the way he handled his bike. The machine fit him as if he'd been born to ride, displaying the same ease as when he rode a horse. Fluid, as if he and the horse were one.

As much as Dana hated to admit it, she looked forward to seeing him again. His gruff, brooding manner had never been a turnoff. She saw him as a challenge, pushing his buttons until he smiled, or on one occasion, turned away in frustration. For whatever reason, she couldn't stop herself from believing he enjoyed their sparring as much as she did.

She followed Kade until he turned onto a dirt road, then parked beside a pristine lake surrounded by low shrubs and tall juniper trees. No tables, fire pits, or facilities. From experience, she knew they'd eat lunch, pack their trash, then turn back toward home within an hour. Most times she'd eat then take a short hike, which is what she planned today.

"Where are you going?" Amber wadded up her wrapper and started to stand when Dana answered.

"Taking a walk. I'll be back in a bit." She took a narrow deer trail through a thick patch of scrub oak, pushing the brush aside until she emerged into a clearing with a sweeping view of the lake. The sun danced off the water as the wind created ripples, pushing the tiny waves toward the shore.

Sitting on a large rock, she picked up smaller, flat stones, trying to skip them across the water with little success. She'd watched her brothers do it when they were young. Although they tried to teach her, she could never get the hang of it. They'd skip once, twice, then sink. Mitch, Kade, and Eric could all skip stones with ease. She guessed it was some rite of passage like shaving for the first time or burping on cue. If you could skip stones then you'd checked off one more qualification for crossing over from being a boy to becoming a young man.

Dana tried once more then decided to head back to the others. She hadn't taken more than a few steps when the sound of motorcycles caught her attention. Knowing the group would never leave her, the noise could mean only one thing. Retracing her steps, she came to an abrupt halt behind some bushes when she spotted a group of riders stopped and still sitting on their bikes. Edging around the tree, she listened to the voices but couldn't make out what was said.

Although they didn't appear menacing, or wear colors as a warning of any affiliation, the longer the other group stayed, the more her stomach drew into a tight knot. Wiping sweaty palms down her jeans, she took a deep breath and a step forward, deciding she needed to move closer. At the same moment, the engines revved, then the sounds of the motorcycles receded into the distance. She dashed toward the others, relieved to see them all standing together, talking.

"What was that about?" Dana's hands trembled before she crossed her arms to still them.

"A group of bikers, like us, out for a ride." Eric saw the concern on her face, the same as he saw on Amber's and Brooke's faces when the group rode up. "Nothing to worry about, Dana. We're all fine."

Her lips drew into a thin line as she nodded. She thought the effects of the ordeal she, Amber, and Brooke experienced a few months ago had ended. Her reaction to the unknown group of riders told her she still had a ways to go to put it all in the past.

"Are you all right?" Brooke put an arm around Dana's shoulders as Amber stopped nearby, her hands clasped in a tight ball in front of her.

"Fine. I was more worried about all of you, knowing I couldn't do much if anything happened."

"As you can see, we're all fine." Kade didn't feel as calm as he let on. He, too, had tensed with the arrival of the riders. Even though he'd spent years working undercover for the DEA in an outlaw motorcycle gang, he could still feel the adrenaline pump through his body, warning signals triggering whenever he saw riders in leathers. More so if they wore colors.

They no longer had anything to worry about. The danger faced months ago had been resolved, even if the emotions still ran high.

"If everyone is ready, we should head back." Eric slipped his hands into leather gloves, his initial state of high alert disappearing as the minutes ticked by. "Dana, you ready?"

She turned the key, sending the others a bright smile. "All set."

By the time they reached the turnoff toward home, she felt relaxed, the initial fear forgotten. It seemed much like when she'd fallen off a horse for the first time. Once she got back on, rode a few minutes, she regained control and her confidence. The appearance of the casual riding group was the same as getting back on a horse. From now on, facing a group of unknown riders would be no big deal—just another day on her bike.

******

Crooked Tree

"My God, Mitch. Are you all right?" Skye jumped off her horse and ran to her brother, crouching as he lay sprawled on the ground.

"Damn that horse," Mitch growled as he pushed into a sitting position, resting his arms across his knees and shaking his head to clear the ringing in his ears.

"Didn't Sean tell you he's green broke and needs a lot more work around cattle? Besides, where's Devil Dancer?" she asked, mentioning his horse.

"Dev's at Reacher Farms. The mare they want to breed is in heat. I took him over yesterday." He dusted off his pants, then stood, stretching his arms over his head. "Damn that hurts. Guess I'm getting a little old to be bucked off."

"I thought you decided not to put him out to stud yet."

"I changed my mind. Jace has been looking for a suitable Grullo for their breeding program. Kade saw Dev when he came to visit last year. We spoke of Dev covering one of their mares while I was at headquarters. I told them I'd see how it goes at Reacher, then decide if I'll trailer him down to Fire Mountain." Mitch watched as one of their men caught the young stallion and walked him over, handing the reins to him.

"I hope you got a good fee for him. Reacher is known to be a tough negotiator." Skye watched as the horse calmed.

"Six hundred."

"Six hundred? That's great. I didn't expect them to pay more than four. You should put some ice on that, old man," she said, watching Mitch limp along.

Looking over his shoulder, Mitch shot her a murderous glare before his mouth turned up into a wry grin. "Old man, huh? Well, this old man is going to ride this young buck until he heels. You're welcome to watch...and learn."

Skye smiled to herself as she swung back into the saddle, riding out of the corral, and reining to a stop before sliding down. Stepping on one of the lowest rails, she leaned over the top, motioning to a couple of the men to join her, ready for the lesson.

"What's Mitch up to?" one of the men asked.

"I believe he's going to impart a lesson to our youngest stallion." No matter what he did, Skye knew he'd handle the horse with a soft touch, continuing the lesson until dark if needed to get the results he wanted. It might take time, but when Mitch finished, they'd have a real fine, although spirited, saddle horse.

******

Four hours later Mitch, Skye, Sean, Samantha, and Rhett sat in the great room of the big ranch house, eating steaks as first Skye, then Mitch, gave their versions of what happened in the corral.

"He bucked you off, huh?" Rhett finished the first of two larges glasses of milk he downed each night with dinner. "How long's it been since you've been thrown?"

"Years, and after hitting the ground today, I don't want it to happen again." He rubbed his shoulder, knowing he'd be taking aspirin and using a cold pack after he ate. "Seems Pop made the right call hiring Jeanie

Naylor."

"I've already scheduled her company for more runs. Either Jeanie or one of her sisters will drive. Cam requested their information for his horse stock group in Cold Creek. I'll send it off to him unless you'd rather wait, see if they continue to do well." Sean finished the last bit of steak, then glanced at the caller ID on his phone. He glanced at the others before answering. "Excuse me."

Mitch turned toward Rhett, ignoring Sean who disappeared into the kitchen to take the call.

"Do you have any interest in working with Skye while on summer break, learning that part of the business?"

Rhett's eyes widened. He'd graduate from high school the following year then leave for college. His father wanted him to continue with classes through the summers so he could finish school early, then attend law school. Rhett didn't know if he agreed with the plan.

"I'd like to but you need to know Pop isn't too fond of me working in the business while in college. He thinks I should concentrate on getting my degree, then go to law school."

"Is that what you want?" Skye asked, already knowing he had doubts.

"It's what he told Pop he wants," Sam interjected, rolling her eyes.

"I want to do what you all did. Work summers in the business, then continue in law school if it's what I decide after getting my degree." Rhett shook his head, looking at Sam as a small grin crossed his face. "I mentioned being a

66

lawyer once to Pop and now he's fixated on it. Because I chose to compete in saddle bronc and team roping instead of bull riding in high school, he thinks I have no interest in the family business."

"But you do." Mitch crossed his arms and leaned back in his chair. He hadn't known how Rhett felt until tonight.

"Getting a law degree doesn't preclude me from working at RTC—at least that's what I believe. What I'm most interested in is our breeding program."

"Then you'll start working with Skye on Monday. You'll need to plan a lot of travel this summer as she's touring some of the bigger rodeos. It'll be good experience for you."

"I'll be happy to show him what we do in accounting." Sam pushed away her empty plate, remembering her last conversation with Rafe. She competed in barrel racing in college, but he felt the same about that event as he did team roping and saddle bronc riding. Since the events weren't connected with bulls, he assumed she had no interest in the family business. He was as wrong about her as he was about Rhett.

"And Pop?" Rhett asked.

"Leave him to me." Mitch decided he might as well add Rhett to his list for Saturday's phone call with Rafe. It would go right at the top, along with Mitch's strong objections to working with the newest member of the marketing team.

He'd heard from Eric about Dana's new job and assignment to the bucking stock companies he and Cam led. Mitch had no issue with improving their marketing, but he wanted it to be Amber, not some newbie who'd argue about every detail. He'd bend on some things, but he'd stay firm on this—Dana would not be a part of RTC's marketing team.

Chapter Six

El Paso, Texas

"Thank you for meeting with me." Matt Garner shook hands, then took a seat across the table from one of the senior executives at Double Ace Bucking Stock. He'd met with Ivan Santiago several times, always in El Paso, and each time noted the two men who milled about, appearing to do nothing except keep watch over Santiago.

"Of course, Matt. It's always a pleasure to see you." Ivan rested his arms on the table, nodding for the two men to leave the room. "What can I do for you?"

Matt handed him a folder containing the latest submitted proposals and recent awards. "These were emailed to you earlier this morning, but I thought you'd like to have them in front of you for our meeting."

Ivan scanned the documents, his brows rising as he read partway down one of the pages. "This is good news, Matt. Much better than anticipated." He continued reading before closing the folder and sliding it back to Matt.

"It's yours. I have a set." Matt should've felt profound satisfaction at what he'd accomplished in less than a year with Double Ace. Instead, he couldn't rid himself of the constant warning in his gut. He'd done a tremendous amount of due diligence on the company before agreeing to their offer and found nothing to dissuade him. Owned by a partnership of two American citizens and a group of Mexican nationals, the company held a strong bank account and the willingness to compete against suppliers who'd been in the business for years.

"Something bothers you. What is it?" Ivan turned to a credenza behind him and poured them each a cup of coffee, handing one to Matt.

Matt didn't know how much to say. His relationship with Ivan began and continued on a quite formal basis, not one lending itself to casual speculation based on a gut feeling. He needed more information before disclosing his concerns.

"Nothing that can't be put to rest by your reassurance."

"And what reassurances do you need?"

"Double Ace has picked up considerable business this year, surpassing my goals and I assume, those of the partners. It's critical we perform well and exceed expectations if we want to obtain renewals for the following season. I just need to know you have the stock available, the people and equipment promised in the bids, and support staff."

"All reasonable concerns. As you know, our stockyards are outside of Houston. You are welcome to visit it anytime, talk with the stock managers and anyone else. You have done well for us, and I don't want your doubts to interfere with continued awards. Shall I make arrangements for you to travel to Houston tomorrow?"

Ivan reached for the phone, then stopped when Matt held up his hand.

"Already done. I'll be visiting them later this week. There is a good amount of up-front money needed to complete the awards. I need to know the funds are there and will be released so there are no delays."

Ivan chuckled, then leaned forward. "Trust me, my friend. Money is of no concern and will be released as agreed to in the contracts. I would not be involved in this business if the funds were not available."

"If I may ask a question?"

"Of course, Matt."

"Why are you involved? Supplying rodeo stock has never been a real lucrative business. If successful, it supports a family, some quite well, but has never made anyone rich. There are so many other ventures to invest money. Why this?'

Ivan's brows knit into a frown, his eyes focusing on the folder in front of him. "Again, a good question. The answer is not so simple." He stood and walked to a window offering an expansive view of downtown El Paso stretching toward the Mexican border. "Double Ace resulted from the desire of the main shareholders to be well connected in the rodeo business. They have plans for further expansion, beyond providing stock."

"You're not telling me much. I assumed there were bigger plans, but that still doesn't explain the amount of investment or the years it will take to capture a majority share of the business." Matt narrowed his eyes. Ivan's response had done nothing except generate more questions.

"Ah, there is much you have to learn about the Mexican culture, my friend. For now, you will have to accept what I have already told you."

Matt knew when a conversation had closed. "It's time I let you get back to your work. Thanks again for seeing me." Matt grabbed his hat and held out his hand.

"My pleasure. I'd like you to join me for dinner tonight, if you have no other plans."

Matt wanted to have a couple beers, eat dinner, then crash at his hotel, not sit through a formal meal with his boss. "Tell me where and what time, and I'd be happy to join you."

******

Crooked Tree

"You certain there's nothing you can do?" Mitch gripped the phone tight, irritation flooding through him. "She's not the right choice for us, Pop."

"Heath, Jace, and I discussed in detail how to make the new plans work. Amber's the director and has the final say. She believes her background and experience in the other divisions fit best, and Dana's complement the stock contracting groups."

"You don't know her as well as I do, and trust me, Dana is not the right person for us." Mitch dragged fingers through his hair, not accepting he'd have to put up with her for days at a time while they worked on updating the marketing plan. "Why don't I get one of the local high school or college kids to set up our social media and update the website? There's no need for her here. She can send ideas to me by email."

"Why don't we cut to the chase, son? You and I both know her experience isn't why you don't want Dana in Montana."

"I don't know what you're talking about."

"The hell you don't. I've seen the way you two are around each other and dislike isn't a word I'd use to describe what goes on between you."

"You're talking crazy. There's nothing going on between us and never will be. She's a pain in the ass and has been since the first day I met her. Let someone else deal with her. I'll get what I need here in Crooked Tree."

The silence stretched between them. Mitch shifted in his chair, waiting for Rafe to respond.

"Make certain this is a battle you want to fight with Heath and Jace. What you decide will impact how they look at you as the company president."

Mitch cursed under his breath. Rafe had hit upon the one flaw in refusing to work with Dana—she already had Heath and Jace's approval.

He scrubbed a hand over his stubbled jaw, a smile spreading across his face as he recognized the perfect solution. If she proved incompetent, unprofessional, or provided bad direction, he'd be able to push her out with the support of all three brothers. He'd wait for her to mess up, then send her packing.

"Fine. I'll work with her, but she better be up to the challenge."

"I haven't seen her back down from you yet."

"She hasn't had to work with me under my terms." Mitch hung up, leaning back in his chair and crossing his arms. If he handled this right, Ms. Ballard would waltz in one door and run out the other. A smug grin spread across his face as he mentally sketched out his plan. The woman who drove him crazy whenever they were together wouldn't know what hit her.

******

Cold Creek, Colorado
MacLaren Rodeo Company

"Other than the minor changes we discussed, your strategy looks good." Cam Sinclair wrote a few more notes in the margin of the presentation before glancing up. "I understand you'll be working with the web design team in Fire Mountain to update all the sites. Does Amber have a complete plan for the social media presence?"

"She does. We worked through it before I left. There are two people on staff with excellent experience setting up social media for previous employers, so we won't need to hire additional people. Once I've met with Mitch and he signs off, we'll be able to start." Dana had no doubt she'd get his approval. All the ideas would improve upon what RTC had done to date. He might have questions or suggestions as Cam had, although she suspected they'd be minor.

"Our office manager has been handling the social media work. You should meet with her to smooth the way as she can be a bit controlling. My suggestion is it would be best to deal with it now rather than after you've started the changes."

"Of course. We don't want to cause friction between us and your team. Besides, I expect we'll be able to incorporate at least some of what she's done into the updated themes."

"I understand Cassie will be giving you a tour of the stockyards and breeding program tomorrow. You might already know we're working with Jace and Kade to incorporate what they're doing in Fire Mountain."

"Amber mentioned there may be some changes in the breeding program, but didn't provide the details."

"Right now we have three separate programs. One for Jace's pleasure riding stock, one in Montana for the bucking bulls, and a third here for the saddle and bareback bucking horses. We're talking about combining them, but there are a number of specifics to finalize."

"I'd guess each is at a different stage," Dana commented as she followed Cam to the door.

"Not as much of a difference as you'd think." He opened the door to the hall, glancing at his watch. "We're meeting Cassie for lunch then I'll leave the two of you to complete the tour."

******

"Do you have any other questions?" Cassie had introduced Dana to most of the employees, showing her the different areas of the stockyard and how they selected stock for the different rodeos.

"I'm certain I will once there's time to absorb all you've shown me. It's a bigger operation than I realized."

"From what I learned from Mitch, RTC is about the same size. When do you meet with him?" Cassie secured a gate behind them before heading toward the parking lot.

"I fly out on Friday."

"Have you met anyone other than Rafe and Mitch?"

"Just at Eric and Amber's wedding. Any input on them would be great." Dana followed Cassie to her truck. "Are you heading out?"

"Actually, we both are. I'm taking you to another location so you can see what I have planned for some of our free time this week." They climbed into Cassie's truck, then pulled out of the parking lot.

"You truly believe I'll have free time?"

"You will once you see what I have set up."

Cassie turned onto a main road, then took a series of side streets. "About the Montana MacLarens. From what I can tell, Rafe and Mitch are the tough ones. Sean is more like Eric—works hard, makes friends easily, and is somewhat the peacemaker. Skye is a lot like me. You can decide if that's good or bad," she chuckled, making one last turn. "Samantha is in college in Missoula, but works summers at RTC in the office. Rhett, he's the youngest, may be the smartest, at least that's what Rafe says. He has one more year of high school. I really don't know much about any of them since Dad and Jace didn't communicate with Rafe until about a year ago. The three might never have fixed their conflicts if they hadn't decided to purchase RTC."

"Mitch has never been married?"

"Not that I know about. Why? Are you going to apply for the position?" Cassie laughed at the thought of Mitch and Dana together. She just hoped they'd make it through their meetings without either inflicting damage on the other.

"Not in this lifetime," Dana snorted. "I can't even guess the type of woman he'd be attracted to."

"Someone as gruff as him?"

"Can you imagine? No, I think it would have to be a woman no one would expect. Sweet, kind, with infinite patience and a great sense of humor. Someone who could put up with his attitude and let it roll off her back."

"Guess the pool of women for Mitch would be pretty small," Cassie said, glancing over at Dana as she pulled to a stop by a large pasture and barn with an attached corral. Three barrels in a competition pattern set in the center of the corral.

"Anyway, I figure it's good to have as much background on him as I can." Dana looked out the window, seeing nothing except the land and barn, not paying much attention to the corral. "What's this?"

"It's our new playground while you're in town." She pointed to the lights suspended on tall poles. "Cam said the previous owner of the company set this up for his granddaughter so she could practice barrel racing. She's in college now, and he saw no reason we couldn't use it."

Dana's eyes widened at the implication. "You're kidding? This is for barrel racing?"

"Sure is. Come on. The horses are in the barn and are ready to ride."

Dana looked down at her slacks, blouse, and black pumps. "I'll need to go back to the hotel and change."

"No need. I brought some clothes for you." Cassie jumped out of the truck, then signaled for Dana to follow. "Come on. You're going to love it."

******

Crooked Tree

Dana grabbed her computer case and carry-on, then navigated the stairs from the plane to the tarmac, her muscles groaning in protest with each movement. She and Cassie had practiced every night, plus Friday afternoon. Nothing compared to the exhilaration of working the horse around the barrels, except perhaps riding her Harley.

"Hey, Dana. Over here."

She looked up to see Sean wave at her from beyond the security barrier.

"How was the flight?" He grabbed her bag, then headed to the exit doors.

"Good. Short." She flexed her muscles, trying to relieve the discomfort.

Sean watched Dana, noticing her discomfort. "You all right?"

"Me? Of course. I'm just feeling the effects of Cassie trying to teach me to barrel race. I had no idea how physically demanding it could be."

Sean laughed as he opened the door to a huge red dually. "You need some help up?"

She set her computer case on the floor, glaring up at him, yet her eyes crinkled in amusement. "Heck no. I may be stiff but I'm not an invalid. At least not yet."

He climbed in across from her and pulled into traffic. "I hope you don't mind staying at the ranch house. The stockyards are across town from the airport and most of the hotels. Skye and I thought it would be more convenient to stay close. There's also a car you can use."

"I don't mind as long as it's not an inconvenience."

"Not at all. With Rafe in Fire Mountain, it's just Rhett and Samantha. Both are working at RTC for the summer and are in and out. The refrigerator's always stocked and you'll get the large guest room with private bath." He turned onto a divided highway and pointed ahead. "RTC is up on the right. The ranch house is a couple miles to the left. We'll stop so you can drop off your bag and get settled, then I'll take you to the office."

They continued down a long drive. As they approached a large house with two stories, a familiar looking truck passed them and honked. Sean waved and honked back.

"Was that Mitch?"

"Yep." Sean paused a moment. "Oh yeah, I almost forgot. He stays most nights at Pop's house."

Chapter Seven

Dana tossed her bag on the bed, fuming at the knowledge she'd be sharing quarters with Mitch. For a split second she'd considered trying to find a way to graciously decline staying at the house. Since she'd made no protest when Sean mentioned Rhett and Sam, it seemed too telling to back out once she learned Mitch was part of the deal.

At Sean's suggestion, she changed into jeans, a blouse, and boots. At the last minute she grabbed her baseball cap, figuring to get teased for not bringing along a traditional cowboy hat.

"All set." Dana met Sean in the entry, admiring the collection of western art on all the walls and the handmade furniture throughout the room. "This is beautiful." She let her hand slide across the back of a wooden settee, noticing the details and finish.

"Mitch made it."

Her eyes shot to his at the unexpected comment. "You're kidding. He never mentioned his talent with wood."

"Yeah...well, Mitch has a lot of skills he keeps to himself. The house is full of furniture he's made over the years. Most of the art on the walls are his, also." He pointed to one a few feet away of a running stream surrounded by tall pines and a peaked mountain in the background. "This is his favorite, just don't tell him I told you. He can be sensitive about his artwork."

"Mitch, sensitive? That's a new one."

"Oh, he has a whole other side few people see. As in, maybe four or five. You ready?"

Within ten minutes they walked into the entrance of RTC. She glanced about, seeing no sign of Mitch's artwork or furniture.

"He's probably upstairs in his office."

She followed Sean, seeing posters of their animals bucking off some of the biggest names in the PBR. Dana already knew about the Professional Bull Riders association and that RTC supplied stock used at their events. There were other, smaller rodeos that contracted with RTC, and she hoped to focus more marketing on those groups. Their breeding program would also receive attention as the MacLarens raised and sold a couple hundred bulls each year.

Sean knocked once on Mitch's door then pushed it open. "Dana's here." He stood aside, nodding for her to go on in.

An unexpected tightening in her chest caught Dana by surprise when she took her first look at Mitch in weeks. At that moment, all she could remember was the searing kiss the night before he left—the one which caused her more than a few restless nights. She let her gaze wander from the hand-tooled belt, to his broad chest and shoulders, settling on the full mouth she couldn't get out of her mind.

"Are you going to stare at me all day?"

She tore her gaze from his lips to his eyes, seeing the humor as well as a knowing look, as if he'd read her mind. Clearing her throat, she reached her hand toward him.

"It's good to see you, Mitch."

He walked around the desk, glancing at her hand then back up to her face before grasping it. Pulling her toward him, he stopped short of touching his body with hers. He leaned down, something almost feral showing in his eyes.

"It's good to see you also, Dana." He held her hand a moment longer than needed, then let go, not stepping away. "Thanks, Sean."

Sean stood silent, watching Mitch act in a way he'd never seen. At that moment he knew, without doubt, his brother had plans for Dana Ballard, but had no idea what. He just hoped his brother didn't mess up with a woman their father and uncles thought well of, screwing up relationships between the companies.

"Sure. Let me know if you need me to show her around."

"Oh, I think I'll be able to do that just fine." Although his words were meant for Sean, he never took his gaze off Dana. Neither heard the door close as Sean left.

She took a breath and tried to step away, almost tripping over a chair leg before he reached out and grasped her arm.

Clearing her throat, she looked up, seeing his steel-gray eyes turn dark, assessing her as if making a decision.

"Thanks. I can be a little clumsy sometimes," she breathed out, feeling him draw her closer. One second she stood a foot away, the next he'd pulled her flush, his head lowering until his mouth claimed hers. He gave her a chance to step away. Instead, she moved her hands to rest on his arms, leaning into him.

She'd yearned for this since he'd left, wanting to know if her body would again respond to him the way it had that night. Refusing to listen to her inner voice saying she should push away and stop the insanity before it got out of control, she wrapped her hands around his neck and held him to her, letting his mouth do wicked and delicious things to hers. It felt as if an electric shock scorched through her body, rocking her all the way to her toes. She moaned aloud a moment before he pulled back. Staring into her eyes, he set her aside.

Crossing his arms, a self-satisfied grin on his face, he stepped away. "You greet all the men at work like that?"

She felt her face color and body stiffen at his obvious insult. Instead of taking the bait, she took a calming breath and mimicked him, crossing her arms, glaring at him as she took a small step forward.

"Forgetting for a moment you were the one to start it, I must say, you seem to have lost something since you left Fire Mountain. Guess you're losing your touch." She turned her back to him, picked up her computer case, and took a seat, noticing he hadn't moved. "Well, you ready to work or do you want a do-over, see if you can improve?"

Mitch narrowed his eyes and dropped his arms to his side, the corners of his mouth turning upward. "Well, babe, from your response, I don't believe I've lost a thing."

"Well, I can't help it if you're delusional. And don't call me *babe*."

He shook his head, taking a seat, and folding his hands on top of his desk. "I understand you're here to convince me we need a new marketing plan, updated website, and added presence on those social media sites I detest." He sat back, clasping his hands behind his head. "So start convincing."

******

Mitch waited for her to fire up her computer, noticing the slight tremor in her hands, and chastising himself for his impulsive action. He'd done the same in Fire Mountain. Something about Dana set him off in all the wrong ways, and even though he knew better, he couldn't seem to stop his need to touch her, feel her fire rip through him. She felt like sunlight and danger, neither sensation comfortable nor welcome. Mitch had to shut this down, if not today, then soon, and send her back home.

Her voice cut into his thoughts and he realized he'd missed everything she'd said since opening her computer. Blinking a couple of times, he sat straight in his seat, sliding a pad of paper toward him and grabbing a pen. At least he could make her think he'd heard her.

"Would it be better if I printed the presentation out for you?"

Irritation swept through him—at Dana, the purpose of

her visit, and at himself for letting her get to him. "I can see the computer fine. Just keep going."

Working through each idea, how it would be addressed, the schedule, and budget, she became increasingly frustrated at what appeared to be total ambivalence. He asked no questions, nor offered any suggestions or comments, answering her entire presentation with complete silence.

After closing her laptop, she set it aside and leaned forward. "What do you think?"

"Interesting. It seems to me you and Amber have gone to a lot of work to fix something which isn't broken."

"That's true. The basic foundation isn't broken, but it can be improved and needs to align with the other MacLaren companies."

"Why is that? We've done fine all these years without changing the brand."

She opened her laptop again, pointing to the updated logos. "As you can see, the basic design is the same. We're updating it to flow with the new marketing material and be consistent with MacLaren Rodeo Company."

"Ah, MRC, the new name for the saddle bronc and bareback stock company. Why go to all this effort when you and I both know RTC will be folded into MacLaren Rodeo within a year."

Although Dana suspected as much, she hadn't been told by Amber or anyone of the proposed change. In her mind, it made sense to integrate as many services as they could, yet she saw little chance of combining the two facilities.

"I haven't been told about moving RTC into MacLaren Rodeo. It does make sense—at least in some of the areas." She slid her computer into the case. "What upsets you about that?"

"Are you kidding?" He pushed back from the desk and walked toward the window, motioning her to join him. "Look out here, Dana."

She moved next to him, feeling her senses go on alert as he brushed an arm with hers.

"You see those men working with the stock? They've been with us since I was a kid. We count on them to keep the business running well, and they depend on RTC for their incomes. The same with the office workers. You and I both know when companies combine duplicated work, people lose jobs, families suffer, and it's almost always an unsatisfactory outcome." He turned toward her, trying to calm his voice, which had hardened with each sentence. "I'll fight any action that impacts my people."

She opened her mouth to speak, stopping when Mitch's phone rang.

Answering the call, he moved away from her, then out into the hall in an obvious move for privacy. Dana turned back toward the window, watching as workers fed the stock and cleaned stalls, walking in hurried motions around the yard. She'd seen the same flurry of activity at Cam's location, although the animals being maintained were horses and not bulls.

As Mitch's absence stretched on, she thought of her

barrel racing lessons and the way Cassie controlled her horse with so little effort. It came from years of experience. Much like riding a bicycle, the skills returned, even if, like Cassie, you hadn't done it in years. She'd competed in high school, dropping off the barrel racing team to concentrate on her studies before going to college.

Dana had no desire to compete, the challenge is what captured her interest. The same as riding her horse, or her motorcycle through winding stretches of mountain roads, and the same challenge she experienced working with Mitch. He tugged at her sense of competence, making her want to prove to him she was as good as anyone else.

"We'll need to meet again tomorrow."

"But—"

"Look, Dana. I know you believe what we're talking about is the most important deal going. Well, it's not. To be honest, it's not even a blip on my scale of importance. I'm meeting with you because I have no choice. On the other hand, you do have a choice—two of them. One, head back to Fire Mountain and we'll communicate via phone and email. So you know, that's the option I prefer. Two, stick around and roll with my schedule."

"I have a flight scheduled this weekend." She hadn't meant to say it out loud and Mitch wasted no time jumping on it.

"Good. Move it up to tomorrow morning." He picked up his hat and opened the hall door. "I'll see you the next time I'm in Fire Mountain." Walking toward the stairs, he paused for only a moment when he heard her footsteps.

"I'm not going anywhere, Mr. MacLaren. You'll just have to get used to me hanging around until you deem it important to finish an assignment handed to us by Heath, Jace, and your father. I'll make myself at home until I hear from you." She walked back into his office, slamming the door behind her, but not before she heard a deep chuckle as he descended the stairs.

******

"I appreciate you checking into this for us, Pop." Skye reread her notes on Double Ace, circling the name of the man she'd lost proposals to over the last few weeks.

"Give me the name and I'll check with Heath and Jace. There aren't too many rodeo contestants they haven't heard of, especially since he's from Arizona." Rafe cradled the phone as he wrote down the name she gave him. "Matt Garner...got it. They're in the valley for the next few days, but I'll get back with you as soon as I can."

"Thanks. Did they take Anne and Caroline down there on a vacation?"

"No, they're meeting with some people who want Heath to run for public office. From the way Jace tells it, they've been after him for a few years. He's turned them down each time."

"So, what's different now?"

"He thinks it may be time to at least listen to the committee. I doubt anything will come of it. Now, how's Dana doing with Mitch?"

"She's no wall flower, that's for certain. It's her first day and Mitch gave her an hour, then he took off for meetings. He warned Sean and me off, saying he'd give her a tour tomorrow before discussing her ideas in more detail. If I were to bet, I think she's got no better than a fifty-fifty chance of winning him over."

"That's better odds than I'd give her. Mitch seems real determined to shut her ideas down flat. 'Course, Heath's already made up his mind to go with what she and Amber came up with. Your brother's got a battle ahead that I'm not sure it's smart to fight."

"It's his battle to lose. You know better than anyone to stay out of his way when he's got something burning a hole in his gut." Skye glanced up as Rhett opened the door and took a seat. "I've got to go. Call me if you learn anything. Love you."

"Was that Pop?"

"Yes. He's going to ask Heath and Jace about Matt Garner...find out if anyone's heard of him. How'd it go today?"

"Emilio never slows down. That guy moves from one fire to the next all day long. He even eats lunch on the run." A wry grin spread across Rhett's face as he spoke about their stock manager.

"He is a whirlwind. At first I wasn't sure Pop made the right move, promoting him after we had to fire Butch, but now I'm a believer. He's done a great job. And letting him hire Fritz as his assistant was a great move." Skye still felt a twinge of pain when she thought of their longtime stock manager who retired and moved to Texas. He'd been with them since before Skye's birth, and she still missed him.

They'd hired a replacement on the recommendation of a local rancher. Turned out Butch had a well-concealed drinking problem coupled with a gambling habit. Within a few months a young bull went missing, along with other items such as an extra set of truck tires, expensive tools, and tack—all objects he could sell to make money. They'd brought in the sheriff and within weeks they arrested Butch for the thefts at RTC as well as from other local businesses. He admitted to stealing the tack and tools while denying any involvement in the loss of the bull. The jury hadn't bought into any of his excuses and sent him off to jail for a few years. Heath made the decision to promote Emilio rather than bring in another outsider.

"What ever happened to Butch? Is he still in jail?" Rhett grabbed a cola from Skye's refrigerator and popped it open.

"No one's mentioned him in a long time. I suspect the sheriff will let us know when he gets out. From what Pop said, he won't be welcome around Crooked Tree." She glanced at her watch. "Well, guess it's time we head out. Did you hear what Dana's doing for dinner?"

"Nope. The last I heard, she drove back to the ranch house to work." Rhett tossed the empty can in a recycle tub and followed Skye into the parking lot. "My guess is she'll grab something to eat out of the refrigerator."

Skye stopped next to her truck, rubbing a hand across her forehead. "I heard Mitch was meeting Lizzie for a drink after work."

"Yeah, right," Rhett snorted. "My guess is he won't be home until late—if he comes back at all."

She glanced at him, rolling her eyes. "Cut him some slack. He's putting in sixteen-hour days and deserves a little down time."

"With Lizzie?"

Skye glared at him, wondering what her seventeen-year-old brother would know about the relationship between Mitch and Lizzie. "It's his choice, Rhett. Don't judge until you're old enough to figure it all out."

"Geez, Skye, from what I've seen in our family, I'll never be old enough to figure it out. Any of it." He pushed his hat down on his head, pulling keys from his pocket. "I'll see you later."

She watched him drive out of the lot, thinking over his last comment and deciding he might be right. Their parents' divorce hadn't surprised them—the reason for it did. Everyone felt relief when their mother moved to Southern California to shack up with her boyfriend.

As far as she knew, their father didn't date, and she certainly couldn't define what Mitch did with Lizzie as dating. Sean's good 'ole boy attitude and charm made him a favorite of the ladies, but he dodged every bullet shot his way. And even though Skye had an on-again, off-again relationship with a college friend, both knew it would never go anywhere. They were buds with benefits...nothing more. As Rhett said, it seemed none of them had figured anything out.

Chapter Eight

Mitch pulled to a stop in the parking area at the front of the house. Turning off the engine, he continued to sit, the aroma of the Chinese takeout he'd purchased filling his truck's cab. The car they'd loaned Dana sat a few feet away, as did Samantha's Jeep. He figured Rhett would be home any minute, starving as always.

He'd met Lizzie at the bar, fully intending to follow her home as he had several times since they'd hooked up again. Intelligent, funny, undemanding, with a knockout body, he figured they'd continue the same as always until she met someone or got one of the jobs she continued to apply for in Bozeman or Missoula. She'd been honest with him about her desire to snag some rich attorney or businessman. He figured it wouldn't take long before she'd be gone. It never occurred to him he might be the one to get crossways over a woman before Lizzie met her sugar daddy.

His meeting with Dana stirred up feelings he wanted to avoid. She rattled him in ways he couldn't begin to understand or defend against. The moment she walked into his office he wanted to drag her to the long leather sofa, strip off her clothes, and claim her. Instead, he'd made a major mistake by kissing her until they were both breathless. The action only fueled his body's already intense reaction to her. Not once in all his years had he felt anything similar for another woman. He couldn't get away fast enough when the phone call came about checking on a new bull.

After two drinks with Lizzie, and without explanation, he'd tossed enough money on the bar to cover their tab and left. Nothing about going home with her felt right, yet nothing about being in the house with Dana gave him comfort.

Clutching the sack of food, he opened the front door, noting the dark kitchen and light coming from under Sam's door down the hall.

"Hey," he knocked. "I've got Chinese out here."

The door burst open. Sam greeted him with a smile. "That's great. I was just trying to decide between making a salad or calling for pizza."

"Do you know if Dana's eaten?"

"It's doubtful. She's been tucked away in the bedroom since I got home. I'll go get her."

Mitch couldn't explain the relief he felt at Sam volunteering to get Dana. He hoped to stay as far away from her as possible, which would be hard living in the same house with her for a few days. If he could get her to leave, he'd be able to find some peace.

Pulling four plates and glasses from the cupboard, he set them on the table, along with the various containers of food and a bottle of wine. Once again the aroma assaulted him as he opened each one, squelching the temptation to dig in. The sound of laughter stopped him, and his gaze swung to Sam and Dana who stopped inside the kitchen, both staring at the food.

"Smells great. Maybe we'll luck out and Rhett won't get here in time." Sam turned to Dana, a devious grin on her face. "He's a huge eater, so it's important you load up before he gets his hands on the food."

Dana nodded, although she hadn't taken her eyes off Mitch since entering the kitchen. She hadn't expected to see him tonight, thinking a man in his position would have meetings or a social function to attend, the same as Heath. A few minutes before Sam knocked on her door, she'd made the decision to drive into Crooked Tree, find a family café and have dinner. The unexpected announcement of Chinese food had her mouth watering. Now, letting her gaze settle on Mitch, she didn't feel even the slightest hunger pang. At least not for food.

"Take a seat and we'll start. No use waiting for Rhett and letting it all get cold." Mitch shifted his stare from Dana, taking a seat on one side of the table, across from where she pulled out a chair. As before, in his office, he needed to put a barrier between them, reduce the chance he'd again do something foolish.

They'd started passing the containers when the front door creaked open then closed.

"Hey, is that Chinese food I smell?" Rhett set his hat on a table as he entered the kitchen.

Sam groaned, putting an extra helping of noodles on her plate before handing the container to Dana, giving her a conspiratorial wink. "Remember what I said."

"You started without me?" Rhett picked up a carton and dished out a healthy portion of orange chicken.

"We're making sure we each get our share, little brother." Sam arranged her chopsticks, then snagged a piece of beef with broccoli.

Minutes passed in silence before Rhett grabbed a carton of milk from the refrigerator and filled his glass. "I thought you had a hot date with Lizzie tonight."

Mitch looked up, glancing at Dana, then shifted his hard gaze at Rhett. "I don't believe I mentioned it to anyone."

Rhett sat down, rubbing the back of his neck as he tried to remember where he'd heard about Mitch's plans. "Sean overheard your conversation with her. I know it's none of my business."

"Damn straight it isn't. But to enlighten you, Lizzie is just a friend."

"Right," Rhett snorted. "Like Skye's *buddy* is just a friend."

"I don't think Dana has any interest in learning about either Mitch's or Skye's friends. Right?" Sam asked, looking at Dana.

"Oh, I don't know. I'm finding the discussion pretty informative." Dana picked up her glass of wine and took a sip, glancing over the rim at Mitch, noting his tight expression.

"Well, in that case, Mitch and Lizzie have this understanding—" Rhett started.

"That's enough." Although Mitch kept his voice low,

controlled, there was no mistaking the rebuke in the tone.

Rhett looked away, realizing what he thought of as messing with his oldest brother had gone too far. "Sorry, Mitch. I'll keep my mouth shut."

"Good idea."

******

For the rest of the meal the conversation centered on work topics, all mention of Lizzie halted. Still, Dana couldn't help wondering about the woman and Mitch's relationship with her. She'd had the impression there were no women in his life, at least no one important. Thinking about it now, she realized a man like him—single, handsome, smart, and wealthy—would have a string of women vying for his attentions. It would be complete folly for her to feel something for a man who had so many options. Especially one with the demeanor of a porcupine. She smiled to herself, speculating there might be another side to the man, one she'd never seen.

"What are you grinning at?"

Mitch's question startled her. "I...uh..." She swallowed a sip of wine as his gaze bore into her, making her want to squirm in her chair. "I was wondering what Crooked Tree is like. Perhaps I'll go out tomorrow night and do some exploring."

"I'm sure Skye would love to take you out with her friends. They know all the great spots for meeting eligible men..." Sam's voice trailed away. "I still have a couple years before I'll be able to go with her."

"Thanks, Sam, but I'm sure she wouldn't want me tagging along."

"Are you kidding? She loves showing people around." Sam pulled her phone out of her pocket. "I'll call her and ask."

"Dana has plans with me."

Dana turned toward Mitch, who now leaned against the counter, arms crossed, his face a mask.

"I don't recall you asking?"

"Well, I am now, and I'm taking you out on Wednesday."

Dana opened her mouth to respond, then snapped it shut, deciding there were worse ways to spend a night than being escorted around town by a prominent local.

Rhett and Sam exchanged glances before Rhett spoke up.

"I'm bushed and I know Skye has a big day planned for me tomorrow." He picked up empty containers and dumped them in the trash. "I'll see you folks tomorrow. You coming, Sam?"

"Um, yeah. See you guys in the morning."

Mitch scarcely noticed the two walk down the hall to their rooms, all his attention fixed on Dana. The thought of her going out with Skye, meeting other men, possibly going home with one, set off warnings he didn't want to explore—at least not yet. The impulsive invitation surprised him, but it felt right in a way he couldn't describe.

Dana stood, picking up her plate and rinsing it before turning toward Mitch, emotions warring inside her. She crossed her arms and leaned against the counter.

"You know, this probably isn't a good idea."

"Don't know why not. We both have to eat." He took a step toward her, keeping his hands at his sides.

"Don't be thick. You know what I mean." She held her ground, even though the butterflies in her stomach threatened to distort her good sense.

"The way I figure it, you've decided to stick around, see if you can find a way to sway me toward your position. Dinner seems to be a reasonable first step." He reached up and slid a strand of hair behind her ear, noticing a tremor at his touch.

She licked her dry lips, then looked away in an attempt to avoid the intensity in his eyes at the same time a warning voice whispered in her head. Taking a deep breath, she stepped away, giving her body space from the heat radiating off his.

"You're saying the dinner is a chance for me to argue my case, get you to change your mind and approve the changes. Nothing more?"

His gaze leveled on hers. "It can be whatever you want, Dana. Business or pleasure. Or both."

Clearing her throat, she moved around him before turning and shooting him a playful grin. "Definitely business, big guy. I'll look forward to it." She turned away without another word, heading for the solitude and safety of her room.

******

"I can't believe we lost another bid." Skye turned her laptop around so Mitch could see the email announcing the rodeo committee had selected Double Ace. "Damn that group. There's no way we can undercut them."

"All we can hope is they don't perform." Sean sat next to Mitch, glancing over at the message.

"We have to do more than that." Mitch agreed with Skye about the money. They'd trimmed as much as they could to still make a profit. There wasn't any fat left. "We need to find out what they're offering. We're losing bids to rodeos we've supplied stock to for years. There must be more to this."

"And how do we do that? They turn me down flat when I ask about Double Ace. Even people I consider friends offer nothing. It's all so frustrating." Skye opened her refrigerator, taking out waters for each of them.

"There must be one person who's willing to speak with you off the record." Sean hadn't worked with the rodeo committee since Skye came on after college. Even though it had been just a few years, the way the groups operated had tightened considerably, not allowing members to discuss the terms of competing proposals.

"Most committees have policies about not sharing bid information. They're getting pretty strict about it, especially the big name venues." Skye pulled a list from the top drawer of her desk and scanned the columns. "That makes five we've lost for next season. We've picked

100

up two, so we're down three and all are smaller rodeos. So far, we haven't lost any of the big ones." Picking up a red pen, she put check marks next to certain names on the list then looked up. "There are five people who *might* talk to me. All have committed to us for the upcoming year, but I know they reviewed bids from Double Ace before making a decision."

"The good news is we're still delivering to a good many rodeos through this summer, including partnering with some bid winners." Sean took the list Skye held out to him. "How accurate is this list?"

"Good, except I haven't had much time to check for new venues over the last year. Updating the list might be a good job for Rhett."

Skye looked up as the door opened and Rhett walked in. "Hey, I have a new project for you."

"Sounds good. Mitch, Emilio says he needs to speak with you and Sean right away. He's next to the pens with Fritz."

"Let's talk about this again after lunch. I want to know what we can do and how soon." Mitch walked out, followed by Sean, Rhett staring after them.

"What's that about?" he asked Skye.

"Have a seat and I'll explain."

******

"Do you know where Emilio is?" Mitch asked one of the stock hands after not spotting either Emilio or Fritz outside.

"The last I saw, he was on the phone in his office." The man nodded toward the portable building used by the stock manager and his assistant.

Mitch and Sean climbed the steps then walked inside, getting a blast of cold air from the wall unit. "Rhett said you need to talk to us."

"I've got some bad news. Seems three of our bulls tested positive for steroids."

"Dammit," Mitch roared the same time his fist hit the desk. "That's not possible."

"That's what I told them, but they did two tests on the ones who tested positive. All the others tested clean. This came by email." Emilio handed Mitch the test results. "As you can see, they're fining us and not letting the bulls compete until they test clean. They've notified the association."

Both Mitch and Sean cursed at the news, knowing there had either been a major mistake in the testing or someone had injected the bulls without their knowledge. Either way, something was terribly wrong.

Mitch stood, pacing back and forth in the small space, then raking a hand through his hair. "Pop and the partners used steroids for a brief time, but that had to be at least fifteen years ago, long before it was banned. As I recall, they did it one year and stopped, figuring any risks to the bulls weren't worth it."

"Have we ever had a bull test positive?" Sean asked.

"Not one, until now. Hell, first some of our best bulls

contract food poisoning, now this. I've never heard of three bulls from the same contractor testing positive. Hell..." Mitch glanced at Sean, remembering his suspicions that someone had tampered with the stock. "Emilio, we need to post men around the stockyard 24/7. I don't know how, but someone's getting to the bulls. I'll take the tests results to the office and call the rodeo chairman, explain our position and see what can be done. Sean, you and Fritz search the medical supplies and log. See who signed in and out, then contact Doc Wheaton, ask Gayle to come out here and check every bull scheduled to compete within the next month. I can't believe she wouldn't have spotted something before the last group went out."

"It's not the doc's fault she didn't find it. One injection given just before loading could've been enough to taint an animal and disqualify him. Injections could even have been administered at the rodeo grounds." Sean pulled his phone from his pocket. "I'll see if she can come out this afternoon to start."

"From now on, we're extra vigilant, even if we have to post a man to each damn bull." Mitch slammed the door as he disappeared outside, taking long strides toward the stairs to his office.

"Mitch? Did you still have time to look at the updated logo?" Dana walked toward him, approaching from the parking lot, her smile hitting him like a punch to the gut.

She'd chosen to work at the house on a couple projects Amber sent, plus the redesign he requested. Anyone else and he would've blown them off, told them to reschedule. Something about Dana haunted him, making him want to keep her close while at the same time push her away. The conflicting emotions exasperated him more each time they were together.

"I have a phone call to make, then we'll talk. Follow me upstairs." He took them two at a time, holding the door open for Dana. "Grab whatever you want to drink. This shouldn't take long."

Dana took a soda from his small refrigerator, holding it toward Mitch to see if he wanted something. He waved her off as he made his call, sitting forward to study the paper he'd laid on the desk.

"Jack Zahn, please."

Dana sat across from him, noticing the deep lines between his brows as he waited for Jack to answer.

"Jack, Mitch MacLaren at RTC. Do you have a minute?"

She stayed silent, hearing Mitch's side of the conversation and guessing at Jack's response from the changing expressions on Mitch's face. Dana knew from listening to Rafe and Mitch that bulls were randomly tested for steroid use with positive tests resulting in fines, loss of prize money, and other sanctions. She also understood there were still some contractors who used the drug, even though it could cause infertility in bulls. A big risk when the contractors stood to make good money in breeding fees after the bull retired from competing.

Mitch stood, pacing around the desk, staring out at

the stockyards, all the while continuing the conversation. By the sound of it, he'd be able to make his point but it wouldn't eliminate the fine or potential stigma of the bulls testing positive.

"Yeah. I'll get back to you when I learn anything more." He looked at Dana, then set the receiver down, letting out a deep breath. "You heard."

"Didn't sound too good. How could something like that happen? Three bulls being injected without someone here knowing?"

"That's what I want to find out. But I'll tell you one thing, no one associated with RTC would ever do this."

"Are you sure?"

He lowered himself into a chair as his mind ticked off all the employees, eliminating them one-by-one. "There'd be nothing to gain."

"Unless they're working for someone else. A competitor might gain from your bulls violating the regulations and being eliminated."

He opened his laptop, punched a few keys, then turned it toward her. "See this? It's a listing of all the stock contractors in the United States."

She blinked at the sheer length of the list. "I didn't realize there were so many. The sources I pulled up showed less."

"This list includes the small contractors, the ones who bid on local rodeos. Regardless, we'd have to say any of them could be behind this. So where do we start?"

She sat back, her lips drawing into a thin line. "I have

no idea."

"Neither do I." He turned the computer around to face him, letting his eyes scan the list. Double Ace jumped out at him, even though he had no reason to suspect them of cheating. He'd never even met anyone from the company and had just one name, Matt Garner. "Excuse me."

Mitch left Dana in his office as he disappeared into the hall. A moment later he reappeared with Skye trailing behind him. She nodded at Dana, then took a seat as Mitch handed her the test results.

"Damn," she muttered, setting the paper back on the desk. "What now?"

"Have you had a chance to find out if anyone knows Matt Garner?" Mitch asked.

"Did you say Matt Garner?" Dana asked, scooting forward in her chair.

"Yeah, you know him?" Mitch narrowed his gaze at her, waiting.

"I know of *a* Matt Garner, but I've never met him. If it's the same one, he's from Fire Mountain. His grandfather, Seth Garner, does most of the construction for MacLaren Enterprises, at least around Arizona. Matt was a bull rider in high school and college. As I recall, he competed in the pros for a while."

"I'll be right back." Skye dashed out of the office then returned, holding out a picture to Dana. "Is this him? It's one of his rodeo promo shots."

"Like I said, I've never met him and didn't see any pictures of him at the MacLaren house."

"Why would they have pictures of him?" Mitch shot a look at Skye, not liking where this might be going.

"Well, if it is the same Matt Garner, he and Cassie were an item for several years. Everyone expected them to marry until Matt took off without a word and entered the pro circuit. None of the MacLarens have seen him since, including Cassie."

"Figure the odds," Mitch muttered, pinching the bridge of his nose between his thumb and forefinger. "Skye, forward the picture to Cassie in Cold Creek. Ask her if this is the same Matt Garner."

"Wait. Send it to Heath or Jace, not Cassie. From what I can tell, she never really got over him, although she tries hard to hide it." Dana looked at the handsome face of the cowboy who'd broken Cassie's heart, making enemies of the entire MacLaren clan in the process. From what she'd heard, it wasn't so much that he broke it off, it was the way he did it—in an email before he hit the road for the circuit. No explanation, just that he was sorry and goodbye.

"I'll get it off to Heath and Jace, and let you know what they say. Thanks, Dana." Skye walked out, leaving Dana feeling as if a hammer were about to be dropped on Cassie. "Why do you want to know about Matt?"

"He's our competition at Double Ace. We've lost five rodeos to them for the next season and we're trying to figure out how, other than the fact they're undercutting everyone."

"I sure hope it's not the same guy."

107

"What's your gut tell you?" Mitch asked.

Her eyes met his, her face void of expression. "That it's the same man."

"Yeah, mine, too."

Chapter Nine

Fire Mountain

Heath looked up from his work and checked the calendar as Jace walked in. "Do we have a meeting?"

"Nope. I wanted to know if you've seen this." Jace held out the picture he'd printed. "I believe Skye emailed it to both of us."

Heath took a quick look at it, a pained expression crossing his face at the image of a boy who'd been like a son to him. The same person who'd broken his daughter's heart.

"Matt. What about it?"

"He's one of the rodeo committee directors for Double Ace Bucking Stock."

"The company who's been taking business away from our rodeo stock groups?" Heath asked.

"The same."

Heath tossed the pen he'd been holding on the desk and sat back. "It's a miracle Cassie hasn't run into him."

"I don't know if she would have mentioned it to us. You know how defensive she is about the way he left. I'm guessing Double Ace has him focusing on the bull stock part of the proposals and another man working on the horse stock and timed events. And the timing may be off. She hasn't been on the job long. In time, I guarantee you she will encounter him."

Heath agreed. He needed to call her, let her know about Matt's job so she didn't get blindsided. "What does Skye want to know?"

"I think she's looking for confirmation he's the same Matt Garner we know. You might want to give Mitch a call, find out if there's more to it." Jace glanced at his phone. "I've got a client to meet in a few minutes. Let me know what you learn," he called over his shoulder as Heath picked up the phone.

"Mitch, it's Heath."

"You got the picture?"

"I did and it's the same Matt Garner who grew up in Fire Mountain. What's going on?"

Mitch explained the sick bulls, positive test for steroids, and they're concerns it may have something to do with Double Ace. He waited for Heath's reaction. When none came, he wondered if he'd disconnected him. "You still there?"

"I'm trying to figure out why Double Ace might target the sabotage at RTC when they're having the same impact on Cam's operation. I spoke with him this morning, and we've lost one contract to them and are in tight competition on several more. The difference is Cam's had no sick horses or drug testing issues. It doesn't sound like a problem with Double Ace, but I could be wrong. Have you spoken with Rafe?"

"Got off the phone with him before you called. He's making some calls before talking with you. His contacts go much deeper than mine."

"All right. I'll wait for him to let me know what he's found out." Heath hesitated a moment, trying to decide how much else to say. "How much do you know about Cassie and Matt?"

"Only what Dana told us. She asked that we not contact her, but go through you to identify the photo."

"She gave you good advice. I want to get in touch with Cassie before she learns about Matt from anyone else."

"No problem. I'll wait to hear back from you or Pop."

Heath hung up, knowing his next call should be to Cassie. He pulled out the bottom drawer of his desk, pulling out a picture he hadn't looked at in a long time. Cassie and Matt with him and Annie at a baseball game in the valley, taken a few months before Matt dropped the bomb and disappeared into the world of pro bull riding.

Heath wished Matt had disappeared some place where Cassie didn't have to see him on the television or YouTube. It had been through his deep friendship with Matt's grandfather, Seth, that the MacLarens and Garners continued to stay friends. Everyone thought Matt had bungled the breakup by not explaining himself to Cassie in person. Even Seth thought he'd taken the coward's way out, and Heath didn't dispute it. Looking at the picture another moment, he set it down and picked up the phone, deciding it best to get this call over with now.

******

Mitch studied the updated marketing material, having put Dana off longer than he intended. Even though he still wanted her gone, other issues required attention, prohibiting his ability to spend much time with her. Maybe they could finalize the work today, have dinner tonight, then he'd put her on a plane.

"What do you think?" Dana asked, her eyes lighting up when she noted the interest he showed in her work. Knowing it ridiculous, she decided to accept any small gesture of approval from him she could get.

"These capture what I had in mind." He pointed to two.

"I agree. They work well with what Cam approved for his group and they integrate with the MacLaren Enterprises logo. Does either one work, or do you have a preference?"

He studied them a few more minutes, finally settling on one where the image popped out against a contrasting background.

"I'll work on the rest of the package today and tomorrow. They should be ready for you to review on Friday, assuming you'll be available."

"Assuming I approve them, what else needs to be done before you return to Fire Mountain?"

"Anxious to see me go, are you?" Even though Dana smiled, making light of his question, a stab of pain struck her at his desire to rid himself of her.

"Nothing personal. We're both buried with work, and

I'm sure you'd like to get back home to your boyfriend."

Her brows drew together. "Boyfriend?"

"You know, the buff, handsome, smart, and eligible attorney." His condescending tone irritated Dana, yet there's no way she'd let Mitch know.

"I'm not seeing him any longer." Picking up the drafts, she slid them into a case and stood. "I'll start working on the changes now and do my best to get them ready for you by tomorrow afternoon. If approved, I'll be on the first plane out Friday morning. Will that be good enough?"

"Sure, that'd be fine." Once the words were out, he knew they were a lie. The knowledge she no longer dated the attorney shouldn't matter, yet it did.

Even though he didn't want anything permanent, her leaving felt wrong. Exploring the obvious attraction between them might stop the way she messed with his mind. A few nights with her and Mitch would be ready to see her leave. Dana was a distraction he couldn't keep around for long.

"All right. I'll make an appointment for tomorrow afternoon." She grabbed her computer and file, heading for the door.

"We'll leave for dinner at seven. Casual."

"With everything going on and my deadline, perhaps we should forget it this trip. Maybe if I come up again—"

"I invited you to dinner and that's what we'll do. See you tonight."

Dismissed, she closed the door behind her, deciding her efforts weren't for naught. He liked the designs and would approve them, she felt certain of it, even if their working relationship continued to feel strained. Driving back to the ranch house, she mentally ticked off what needed to be done for their meeting the following afternoon. There remained a number of items he needed to approve, including website elements as well as the scope and direction of the social media program.

She'd said nothing to Mitch about their website, which hadn't been updated in years. Skye added to the list of rodeos as they obtained new contracts, but other than that, no one seemed to touch the site. Once the elements were approved, all changes could be made in Fire Mountain.

Dana pulled to a stop in front of the house and reached for her phone. Searching her contacts, she found the number for the MacLaren executive assistant.

"Hi Phyllis, it's Dana. I need plane reservations to return to Fire Mountain on Friday. Yes, that's right...I guess around ten or eleven. Thanks, you're the best."

The house seemed so quiet, and large, with no one else around. She poured a diet soda into a glass filled with ice, grabbed a bag of chips from the counter, then set up her computer on a game table in the family room. Amber would correct her by calling it a great room, like the one in Heath and Annie's house. Either way, the room invited you to make yourself comfortable and enjoy the beautiful furniture and art.

She ran her hand along the edge of the table, guessing Mitch had been the creator. Waiting as the laptop fired up, she scanned the walls. Five more pieces with his signature graced the large space, all landscapes with impressive colors and dimension. She wondered if he painted on location or used photographs, or even by memory to create art she considered better than what could be seen in many galleries. Dana made a mental note to ask Mitch about them at dinner.

Her throat convulsed as she thought of time alone with him. Gatherings with friends hadn't posed a problem. They spoke and sparred as would any two people who enjoyed pushing each other's buttons. When the two of them were alone, everything changed, and her desire for him thundered beyond any rational thought. Never in her life had she ever experienced such an intense attraction for a man.

She'd noticed his strong hands, muscled arms, and sculpted chest when he'd helped around the MacLaren ranch and which he now hid under long-sleeved shirts. Skye told her he worked out several times a week, ran at least two mornings, rode his horse, and took out his Harley as much as possible. It sounded like the same routine as when he lived in Fire Mountain. She wished they had time to ride during her visit in Crooked Tree—horses or bikes or both, she didn't care.

What she longed for was a chance to get to know Mitch, peel back the layers and learn how someone so moody and brooding could also create such emotionally charged art using wood and oils. He had to be the most talented man she'd ever met. Instead of always walking into an uneasy truce, she wished for a normal conversation between two people, if for no other reason than to see where it would lead.

******

"You look wonderful." Mitch stared at Dana. Freshly showered, she stood before him in a simple marine blue silk blouse over tight black jeans. Her red hair fell in waves around her face and over her shoulders, enhancing her sparkling blue eyes.

After cleaning up, Mitch had slid into a black patterned shirt, jeans with a hand-tooled black leather belt and silver buckle, and black boots. Holding his gray suede jacket, he knocked on her bedroom door, not expecting all the air in his lungs to whoosh out at the sight of her.

"Thank you. You look pretty good yourself." She let her gaze wander over him another moment before picking up her purse and jacket. "Where are we going?"

"A steak and seafood restaurant across town. They always have music, although they mix it up quite a bit." He grimaced when he remembered their Wednesday night schedule. "I hope you're okay with karaoke."

"Are you kidding? I love it, although I'd never get up on stage myself."

He helped her into his truck, taking back roads toward their destination.

Heavy traffic slowed them down, and as the miles

passed, Mitch felt a growing need to reach out and take her hand in his. Instead, he gripped the steering wheel tighter, then turned the air conditioning up to combat the increasing warmth in the truck and heat coursing through his body.

The steakhouse parking lot had no empty spots by the time they arrived. Mitch drove to the back lot, circling twice before crossing a narrow bridge to an overflow area. After pulling to a stop and turning off the engine, he walked around to open Dana's door, assisting her down, even though she needed no help. His hands lingered on her waist for long moments before she glanced up and staggered at what she saw. The cool, detached look she'd come to expect had vanished. Instead, his eyes had turned stormy and confused, as if he fought some unwelcome internal struggle.

Her lips parted a fraction as the play of emotions continued to dance across Mitch's face. For an instant she felt certain he'd bend down and kiss her. Instead, he let his hands drop to his sides and turned, escorting her to the restaurant's back entrance.

"Hello, Mitch. It's been a long time." An older woman, slender with almost white hair, walked up, shooting a curious look at Dana before giving him a hug. "Do you have a reservation?"

"I do." A relaxed smile lit his face, a rare occurrence from Dana's experience.

Scanning the list, she picked up two menus. "Ah, there you are. The alcove table. Good choice." She led them through two rooms, both filled to capacity. Mitch stopped several times to greet other diners and shake hands before the hostess stopped at a booth tucked into a corner under an archway. "Here you are. I'll send your waiter over."

Mitch nodded, stepping aside for Dana to slide onto the seat. Following her, he moved close until his thigh touched hers, then shot her a look, as if daring her to shift away. She stayed put, picking up the menu and scanning the choices as her mind took in the whole scene that had all the elements of a date and not the business meeting she expected.

Dana continued to study the menu as their drinks arrived. "What do you recommend?" she asked Mitch, who didn't bother with opening his.

"I'm getting a ribeye. Their salmon is also excellent— at least that's what I've been told."

They ordered, then sat back to relax and listen to the music coming through speakers installed overhead.

"Do you come here much?"

"First time since I returned." He picked up his whiskey and took a sip while his gaze wandered over her. "That's a good color for you."

"Is that a compliment from Mitch MacLaren?" She smiled, setting down her wine glass.

"I'm known to give one on occasion. Don't get used to it." His eyes crinkled at the corners as his lips tilted up. Not a full smile, but close.

"Tell me about Lizzie." She'd wanted to ask ever since Rhett mentioned her and Mitch almost bit his head off.

He stilled, his face losing all humor. "Nothing to tell. She's a woman I know."

"Ex-girlfriend?"

He snorted. "Not quite."

They quieted as the waiter set down their meals and left. Dana didn't wait, taking a big bite of her salmon.

"Oh, man, this is good." She took a second bite, followed by a third before slowing down to pick up her wine. She glanced at Mitch, noticing he hadn't started. "Is there something wrong with your steak?"

"Uh...no." He cut a slice, realizing he'd been staring at Dana, enjoying the pleasure she took from her meal. He'd never known a woman who attempted so much and enjoyed it all, throwing herself full force into everything. "What happened with your attorney?"

She stopped chewing and thought of Kell, a smile playing at the corners of her mouth.

"We're still friends. It just didn't go any further. Tell me more about Lizzie."

"Nothing to tell. I've known her since high school. We're friends." He shifted in the seat, his eyes fixed on the plate in front of him.

The twisting sensation in her stomach at his answer surprised Dana. No reason existed for her to feel even a slight bit of jealousy over any woman. She didn't ask him to clarify his answer. Her instincts told her exactly the type of friendship he shared with Lizzie.

"She's looking for a job in Missoula. It's doubtful I'll see her much."

Dana didn't know why she cared one way or the other. The odds she'd see Mitch more than a handful of times each year were slim. She pushed her plate away at the same time he finished the last of his steak.

"Do you want dessert?"

She rested hand on her stomach and grinned. "Not this trip."

"Good. Let's get out of here."

Chapter Ten

"Before we go back to the ranch house, I need to stop at my place to pick up the mail and make sure everything is okay. Unless you need to get back sooner." Mitch glanced at her, then shifted his gaze back to the road.

"Stopping by your place is fine. Besides, I wouldn't mind seeing how you live."

"Don't expect a big house like Rafe's or hundreds of acres." He sounded defensive, as if she'd judge him by the size of his home.

Ignoring his comment, she changed the subject as he turned onto a paved road, the lights of a house appearing in the distance. "Have you ridden your bike lately?"

He shot her a quick glance, his mouth pursing. "Nope. There hasn't been much time. I hope to ride this weekend with a group of guys I've known since high school. I heard you bought a new bike."

"A deal I couldn't pass up. Two years old, low miles, and no modifications needed. He fits me better than any bike I've ever owned."

"He?"

"Well, of course. You don't expect me to straddle a female bike do you?" She bit her lower lip, trying not to smile when Mitch let out a bark of laughter.

"No, I certainly wouldn't recommend it. Do you have a

name for this male bike?"

She thought a moment about her answer, remembering a phrase her grandmother used to use when faced with a difficult decision. *In for a penny, in for a pound*, she'd say. The thought pushed Dana to answer his question with the truth. "Mitch."

His gaze shot to hers before he slammed on the brakes in front of his house and killed the engine.

"You call your bike Mitch?" His already deep voice held a huskiness she hadn't noticed before. He turned toward her, an arm resting on the seat back, his eyes intensifying as they locked on hers.

She caught her lower lip between her teeth, then moistened her dry lips, trying to create distance between them by sliding toward the passenger door.

"Yes. It seemed appropriate. He's a little moody sometimes, takes some effort to start on cold mornings. With the right words and proper encouragement, he does fine."

The woman is trying to kill me, Mitch thought at the same time his hand snaked out and grabbed her wrist, pulling her toward him.

"And what do you do if he refuses to respond?" His warm breath fanned her face.

"I...um..." Her voice trailed off as she focused on his full lips a scant inch away from hers. She wanted them on hers again, creating heat and sending the same waves of delicious warmth through her body as he'd done before. When she thought he'd drop his hold and pull away, he drew her forward, capturing her mouth with his.

Showing no hesitation, she wrapped her hands behind his head and pulled him down in a crushing kiss as a hand splayed across her back, the other at her neck. The kiss turned demanding, persistent, her body arching toward him. His hands moved under her blouse, exploring the soft lines of her back and waist.

She moaned as his tongue explored the hidden recesses of her mouth, while a hand slid from her back to her stomach, strong fingers teasing, moving upward. Her emotions whirled as pleasure radiated outward. Breaking the kiss, she gasped for air, her fingers tracing a path down his cheek to his stubbled jaw and across his bottom lip, placing a soft kiss on his chin.

He gripped her chin between his fingers, holding her steady, his mouth descending to meet hers, coaxing her to open once again. Her body tightened even as she melted into him, her hands gripping his arms as if she feared he'd back away. Instead, in one fluid move, he reached under her, settling her on his lap, and deepened the kiss.

Cradling her in his arms, he let a hand move down to her calf, then slowly upward to her thigh and hips, feeling heat radiate, even through her clothing. His hand continued upward to her back, feeling her fevered skin as his mouth continued to devour hers. He drew away, sucking in air, his forehead resting against hers.

"Let's go inside," Mitch rasped out, his heart pounding so hard he knew she must also be able to hear it. He set her aside, taking a shaky breath as he climbed out, grabbing Dana's hand to help her down as she slid over. They wasted no time getting inside, Mitch kicking the door shut. He drew her to him and took her mouth with his, picking up where they left off.

Mitch unbuttoned the top of her jeans at the same time she did the same to his. The sight of her small hand reaching for him caused his mouth to go dry. Gripping her hand, he stopped her movement, pressing it tight to his thigh, his eyes locking with hers.

"Dana, make certain this is what you want. I'm not a great bet for anything more than short term. I don't want you to regret this."

She saw the need in his eyes, feeling the same desire course through her. *If she had just one night with him, would it be enough or would she expect more?* The certainty she'd want more rocked her as well as the realization she'd take whatever he offered and deal with the consequences later. Her gaze lifted to his, a hand spread across his chest.

"I want this, Mitch."

"All right, but I'm telling you now, one time in my bed tonight won't be enough."

She leaned toward him, placing a heated kiss on his lips. "Of course not. It's just the appetizer."

******

Dana lay cradled in Mitch's arms as the early sun cast rays of light through his bedroom window. His deep breathing washed over her face, a feeling of contentedness she'd never known wrapped around her. Spreading a palm, she played with the crisp hairs of his chest, turning her face to trace a sensuous path along the taut muscles. Letting her hand move ever lower, she gasped when a hand shot out to still her path.

"You're going to kill me, you know." The deep, morning rumble of his voice sent chills through her body as she gazed up to look into intense, sleepy eyes. He pulled her up onto his chest, taking her mouth for a leisurely kiss, aligning her body with his.

They'd had the hottest sex of her life on the sofa in his living room, then in his bed before he picked her up and carried her to the shower. Afterwards, he'd wrapped her in one of his robes, took her hand, and walked into the hall for a brief tour.

Although he stayed at Rafe's most nights while his father worked in Fire Mountain, his own home appealed to her on a personal level. The two stories with a wrap-around porch and central courtyard seemed cozy and traditional. The full moon allowed her to appreciate how it faced lush meadows in the front and imposing mountains in the back.

Afterwards, he'd lifted her once more into his arms and set her down on his magnificent bed with hand-carved head and footboards. Making love until their bodies could take no more, they finally slept until she woke at dawn.

Breaking the kiss, he rolled out of bed, tossing her an

oversized t-shirt before scavenging for food in a kitchen ill-used the last few weeks. She didn't know why it surprised her when he whipped up a quick meal of eggs, hash browns, and bacon. Food had never tasted as good.

When they finished, he took her by the hand, walking toward the bathroom, and turning on the water.

She'd used it last night, but didn't fully appreciate the oversized shower with two heads, oval whirlpool, and vanity with a granite top over the most beautiful cabinets she'd ever seen.

"Did you make these?" She ran a hand over the sleek wood, noting the bronze handles.

Mitch nodded. "Once we buttoned up the house, I finished every bit of the inside. It took a few years, between work and travel, but I got it done." He tested the water, then drew her under it with him.

Wrapping her arms around his waist, she looked up and smiled. "I don't believe I've ever seen a lovelier home. It's magnificent." She rested her head on his chest, feeling him tighten his arms around her.

Mitch rested his chin on the top of her head, knowing he had to let her go, tell her what they had last night and this morning wouldn't last. Relationships and a belief in love weren't in his nature. He could have sex with her until they were both totally spent and enjoy every moment without ever committing to more. In his world, people weren't faithful and no manner of vow could change human nature. Men and women were predisposed to cheat on each other—it wasn't a matter of if, but when.

He lived in a world of darkness and distrust, while Dana radiated light and hope. Life with him would do nothing except drag her down, drown her in his disgust for what he knew to be the true nature of love and relationships. Loving him would serve no purpose except snuff the radiance and warmth out of her, and it would kill him to watch that happen.

"We should get moving," he whispered, tightening his grip while letting his arms fall to his sides.

They finished, each soaping the other, resisting the urge to make love once more before returning to real life. As he dried Dana, then wrapped her in one of his oversized towels, he cursed himself for what he believed, deep in his soul, to be true about men and women, and their inability to be faithful.

"Are you ready?" He pulled on his boots, then stood, watching as she finished buttoning her blouse. He'd never get enough of her and accepted he had no choice except to let her go.

She drew fingers through her hair, trying her best to get rid of the thoroughly loved look.

"What will they think?"

Mitch's brows drew together. "Who?"

"Sam and Rhett. They know we went to dinner and never came home. Now we'll be driving to the office about the same time. What should we say?"

"Nothing. It's none of their business. Besides, you'll be leaving tomorrow. End of story." He grabbed his hat, trying to ignore the flash of pain he saw cross Dana's face or the tightening in his own chest. "I'll drop you at the house so you can pick up your computer then drive in, unless you prefer to work there until we meet this afternoon."

Dana swallowed the lump in her throat as well as the unbidden pain his comment caused. As it turned out, their time together meant nothing to him except another one night stand. After she left, unpacked, and spent another night in her apartment, he'd be back with Lizzie, perhaps taking her to dinner and for a drive afterwards. *Stop it*, she cautioned herself before turning toward him.

"Did you say something?" Mitch asked, waiting by the door.

"Just that I believe I will work at the house and drive to the office this afternoon for the meeting." She averted her gaze, pretending to search for her purse when she knew it sat in the same spot as last night.

After the night they'd spent together, the silence on the way to the house choked her. She wanted to scream at her stupidity, believing what happened between them might be the start of something special when it was just sex. She took a deep breath, staring out the window at the passing scenery, deciding her best course of action was to act as unaffected as Mitch. Straightening her back and clutching her purse, she jumped out as soon as Mitch pulled to a stop, not turning when he called her name. The fantasy had morphed into reality and she had to accept it.

******

Mitch let loose with a stream of curses as he turned the truck around and drove to the office. If only he could take back his thoughtless comment, sit down with her and explain. Instead, he'd smacked her with his flippant response, trying to push her away, and succeeding. Turning onto the highway, the reality he already missed her hit him in the chin like a knockout punch. Wrenching the steering wheel to the right, he pulled to a stop on the side of the road, slamming his fist onto the dash.

Rubbing his eyes with the palms of his hands, he muttered another oath at the sound of his phone. He swiped a finger across the screen and brought it to his ear.

"MacLaren."

"Mitch, where are you?"

"Something wrong, Sean? I don't remember having any appointments."

"You don't, but we have another situation. Something happened last night at the far corral. A section of fence broke and we're missing four of our young bulls."

"I'm on my way." Forcing thoughts of Dana from his mind, he pulled back onto the highway, focusing his energy on where it should have been from the start, on the business. Pulling into the lot, he spotted the sheriff's car and noticed a group of men huddled outside the office.

"Hey, Mitch. Over here." Sean motioned for him to join them, then turned his attention back to the sheriff, his deputy, Emilio, and Fritz.

"Sheriff." Mitch extended his hand.

"Mitch. Seems you're plagued with problems of late."

He nodded, looking at Emilio. "Did you find them?"

"We did. They couldn't go far and are already secured in another area."

Mitch let out a breath. At least they'd been found. "Show me where they got out."

Skye and Rhett joined the group who walked the length of the property to the most distant corral. One section of wooden fence lay on the ground, as if it had been trampled. Mitch and the sheriff studied the area around the corral, looking for anything that would give them a clue as to what happened.

Mitch turned to Sean. "Looks to me like the animals spooked and trampled the fence. It may not have been intentional."

"You're right, but I thought it best to get the sheriff out, just in case."

"I see you have a cyclone fence around the perimeter. Is it new?" the sheriff asked Mitch, holding his notepad and pen.

"We installed it about six months ago for situations such as this. Most of the corrals and pens are made of metal tubing, and we've never had a problem. A couple pens, where we keep young bulls, are wood. They're scheduled to be replaced this month. With the cyclone fence, the bulls might get out of the corrals, but they have nowhere to go unless someone cuts the fence."

"It appears to be a simple case of the animals breaking through the fence. If it were an attempt at stealing them, the cyclone fence would be cut. We'll check it all out anyway." The sheriff turned to his deputy, instructing her to take pictures and interview the person who first found the damage as well as anyone who helped round up the bulls. "Do you think it could be a prank? College or high school kids out for some fun?"

"It's hard for me to believe anyone from around here would think letting young bull stock loose would be funny. Most everyone's been raised around cattle or horse stock of some kind. Now, if you're talking city kids in town for a few days, yeah, maybe. Again, I don't think it's likely." Mitch rubbed the back of his neck, agreeing with the sheriff's thoughts about it being a case of animals getting spooked.

"I need to head inside for a conference call, Mitch. It shouldn't take long." Sean took off toward the office as Skye and Rhett continued to circle the area.

Mitch thought of the extra men guarding the area around the clock. "Emilio, do you know what happened to the person assigned to this area?"

"He called in sick, Mitch, and I didn't have anyone to replace him. Fritz was in Bozeman to pick up an order we placed weeks ago. I tried to make the rounds myself. It didn't help much."

"Don't blame yourself, there's a lot going on and we're all working overtime to keep up." Mitch thought of his night with Dana and felt a pang of guilt at not being here with the other men. "Guess I'd better get back to work. Emilio, unless the sheriff needs to look around some more, I'd like you to get some men to fix this right away."

He shook the sheriff's hand and turned toward the office, his mind again wandering to Dana and their night together. It struck him how difficult it would be to forget her and try to convince himself she meant nothing but a one night pleasure. To make matters worse, even now he wanted her again.

The rest of the morning and afternoon dragged on. Mitch could concentrate on his work for only short periods of time before his thoughts would shift to Dana and he'd lose all concentration. They'd known each other for several months during his time in Fire Mountain, joining the others for horseback rides, trips on their motorcycles, and dinners at Heath and Annie's. They'd worked on various projects, including the last week while finalizing the marketing changes. He wondered how any woman could work her way under his skin in such a short period of time, stealing his thoughts, and creating a passion he wanted to forget.

Setting down his pen, he closed his eyes, picturing her smiling at something he'd said early in the morning while chowing down on breakfast. Her sparkling eyes crinkled at the corners, and he'd reached out to wipe a dab of yoke from her chin, licking it off his finger. She'd leaned over, placing a warm kiss on his lips then traced the outline of his mouth with her tongue.

He cursed, standing to gain relief as his body responded to the memory. Grabbing a bottle of water, he twisted off the cap and took a long swallow, wishing he could pour the entire contents over his head.

He'd been a fool to believe one night with Dana would be enough. Hell, a hundred nights wouldn't come close to satisfying his desire for her. Rubbing a shaky hand down his face, he cursed his flawed luck—finding the perfect woman, but knowing he'd be able to commit to nothing more than what they already had.

******

Cold Creek, Colorado

"We're approved as the contractor for the rodeo in Oklahoma." Cassie's enthusiastic voice traveled down the hall and into Cam's office before she stepped inside.

"Congratulations. I know you've been worried about this one." Cam hung up the phone as Cassie sat across from him.

"We may need to bring in one or two sub-contractors. I won't know until I check stock and the event schedule again."

"Bringing in subs doesn't bother me unless we do have the stock required to handle the contract on our own. I'd always prefer to keep the money than split it with others." Cam searched her face, looking for any signs the news about Matt Garner bothered her. "We will need to bring in RTC for the bulls."

"I could always contact Matt to see if Double Ace wants a piece of this." The bitter tone of the words confirmed her displeasure at the news Matt had joined their competition. She thought of the series of events which led to Heath discovering Matt's involvement with Double Ace. Making her aware of the news bothered her father, but she couldn't afford to be blindsided by running into him at one of the events.

"I did some checking. Matt's well thought of in the business."

"At least he's in the bull stock part and not horses." Cassie crossed her arms. "My research indicates Double Ace has a large herd of saddle, bareback bronc stock, bulls, and timed event stock, enough to rarely need the services of other contractors. I'd love to travel to Houston sometime to see their facilities. They must be huge."

"There's no reason you can't. At some point they will need to sub-contract part of the stock and there's no reason we can't be the company they select. You'll need to connect with the person who fulfills the contracts, not the rodeo reps, like Matt. The odds are slim you'd encounter him." Cam picked up a folder he'd recently updated on the company and opened it. "My notes say Gage Templeton is the one you want to meet. He's in charge of contract fulfillment for the entire operation. Maybe it's time to go meet the man."

Cassie sank a little into the chair. Meeting with Gage would be the smart move as MacLaren Rodeo had a stellar reputation in the horse stock business. She might even be able to plant a seed about RTC. The reason holding her back involved Matt Garner and the quite real potential of running into him at Double Ace. Cam didn't need to know the possibility bothered her.

"I wonder if Skye would want to come along. We could meet with Gage, make a pitch for both businesses, and get a good look at their stock and operations." Pushing her concerns aside, she thought of the timing, knowing it would be possible to work a trip into her schedule.

"Do you want to call her or should I?" Cam agreed with her idea. Might as well hit him with both companies at one time.

"I'll call today so she can talk it over with Mitch. We might be able to set it up for some time in the next two weeks."

"Review this to see if there's anything you haven't already learned about them." He slid the folder across the desk.

Cassie wasted no time contacting Skye and securing her interest. Both hoped they could set up a meeting and tour the Double Ace facility right away, before the company made any sub-contracting decisions for the recent contracts they'd secured. Skye had heard of Gage Templeton, and like Matt, he had a clean reputation as both an ex-rodeo competitor and businessman. They needed more, and by the time a meeting took place, both women vowed to learn everything they could about him and Double Ace.

Chapter Eleven

Crooked Tree

Dana parked in the lot, leaning over to grab her computer and files. She spotted Mitch's truck a few spaces away, pushing aside the disappointment at the certainty at how it would end between them. She believed they'd never be together again as they had last night. A vague smile touched her lips—at least she'd have the memory.

"Wait up, Dana."

She waited for Skye to walk up next to her, hoping Mitch's sister hadn't heard anything about last night, or the fact they hadn't made it back to the house.

"How's it going?" Dana reached for the entry door handle, trying to juggle her files and computer.

"I'll get it." Skye reached in front of her and pushed the door open. "Do you have plans tonight?"

"Nothing other than packing to leave in the morning."

"You're leaving so soon? I thought..." Skye stopped when she realized what had almost popped out of her mouth. She knew neither had made it home last night and hoped perhaps Dana and Mitch might have started something that would last a while.

"You thought what?"

"I assumed you had more work to do here. Anyway, a couple of my girlfriends and I are going out for drinks.

Why don't you join us? We all work, so it won't be late."

Dana didn't feel much like going out, although after some consideration, she decided it would be a good way to get to know Skye and keep herself from falling into the funk beckoning her.

"Sounds great."

"Wonderful. Let's meet at the house at six and I'll drive."

They walked up the stairs, Skye ducking into her office as Dana walked the few extra steps to Mitch's. Grabbing the handle, she took a deep breath and walked in, a determined smile firmly in place.

"Hope I'm not too early."

Mitch glanced up, his breath hitching at the sight of her. They'd been together not twelve hours before, naked, tangled in sheets, her back tucked against his chest with him feeling a sense of peace he'd never known. The look on her face this afternoon, a mixture of determination and caution, told him he'd be fortunate to salvage a friendship.

He started to speak, then cleared his throat. "No. Now is fine."

Nodding, she spread the material out on his desk. It had taken eight hours of nonstop work to complete all the elements so she could have them ready for today's meeting and fly out in the morning. Each time she thought of his words, knowing he couldn't wait to get rid of her, she pushed harder, determined to present her best work and leave with her pride intact.

"The revised logo, example of the updated website,

and mockups of RTC's Facebook and Twitter pages." She indicated each one, watching as Mitch looked from one to the other. "The details will be fine-tuned as the work progresses, so don't feel all of this is set in stone. The idea is to be more interactive, keep the content updated weekly, and draw people to the pages."

Mitch hunched over her work, studying each concept, then leaned back. Grabbing a pen, he signed his name to the bottom of the documents and slid them back to her.

"They're approved. Anything else?" he bit out, sighing when he saw Dana wince at his curt words.

Capturing her lower lip between her teeth, she stifled the blunt reply, stacked the pages, and slipped them into her folder. Straightening her spine and forcing her shoulders back, she summoned a forced smile and held out her hand.

"Thank you, Mitch. Once or twice a week I'll send you progress reports and additional work to review. Going forward, we can communicate by email and phone."

Mitch stood, eyeing her outstretched hand. He grasped it, relieved the desk provided a barrier, prohibiting him from pulling her into his embrace. What he hadn't expected was the immediate and intense jolt to his body the contact, her skin to his, triggered. His jaw worked, although words failed him. Releasing her hand, he stepped around the desk, stopping inches away.

"Have dinner with me tonight."

"No." Dana glanced away from his intense gaze, licking her dry lips. "I already have plans for this evening."

"That so?" He continued to stare, letting his gaze wander to her mouth then back up to her eyes, which compared to last night, held none of the brilliance he hoped to see.

"Skye asked me to join her and some friends for drinks."

"Then I'll meet you for dinner afterwards."

Mitch stood so close she could feel heat radiate off him, wrapping around and almost choking her with memories of what his body could do to hers. Taking a step away, she gripped her computer case tighter as she turned toward the door.

"Thanks, but I need to pack. My flight leaves early and I don't want to miss it."

"I'll take you to the airport." Conflicting emotions warred within him. He knew he should let her go. Dragging it out wouldn't change his feelings about love and relationships, and would do nothing except make her leaving more difficult.

Stopping, she glanced over her shoulder, a look of regret passing over her face. "Again, thanks, but no. I have it covered."

The sound of the door closing felt like a blow to his chest. Shoving both hands in his pockets, he let out a deep breath, realizing letting her go might be much harder than he'd ever thought.

******

139

"Hope it's not too loud in here for you." Skye leaned away from Dana, letting her gaze wander to the stage and the next performer. The packed country western saloon offered karaoke two nights a week, drawing locals from miles around.

"Not at all. I can't believe how good some of these people are." Dana sipped her single malt scotch, enjoying the smoky taste as it rolled over her tongue.

"You want to give it a try?"

Dana laughed at the suggestion. "Trust me. If I got on stage, I'd clear the place in thirty seconds."

"I wish my friends could've made it. You'd like them. Next time you're in town we'll all get together and go out. Unless you want to spend all your free time with someone else." Skye saw the change in mood her comment caused and narrowed her gaze on Dana. "You will be seeing Mitch again, won't you?"

Warning signals went off in Dana's head. She had to keep it professional. "Of course, for meetings and perhaps business lunches or dinners."

"I know it isn't my business, but Sam and Rhett mentioned neither of you came back to the house last night. Well, I guess we all wondered if...you know..." her voice stilled at her inept attempt to ask about the two of them.

Dana set her drink on the table, cupping her hands around the glass, deciding how much she should say.

"Look, I know how it must look, but a relationship isn't something we're going to pursue, if that's your question."

"Why the heck not? When Sam said you two didn't come back to the house after dinner, we all thought there might be more to it."

Dana thought the same until Mitch set her straight. She stared into her drink, taking another sip and wishing she could have more time with him. "I'm sure you can understand what is or isn't between us is private. All I'll say is we had a great time with no strings."

"Is it because you're in Arizona and he's here?"

She shifted in her seat, not wanting to talk about Mitch and the fact he'd gotten over her after one night. "Distance has nothing to do with it. It would be irresponsible for me to get involved with the president of a MacLaren company, and to be honest, he's not in the market for anything more."

Skye blew out a breath. She understood Mitch as well as anyone, and the fact he'd gone out with someone from the company, a woman he liked and respected, said much more than what Dana believed. She reached over and put a hand on Dana's arm.

"Mitch is a hard case, which you already know. Give him time. He may surprise you."

As much as Dana appreciated Skye's encouragement, she knew better than to wait for him just because they'd shared one amazing night together.

"Not going to happen. My life is full enough with work and friends. I don't need to put it on pause, hoping he'll change his mind and decide he might want something more." She plastered on a smile, hurting inside for what they might have had together if he could free himself from whatever held him back—and she believed with everything inside her he fought demons deep within him.

"Would you care for a dance?"

Dana glanced up to see a cowboy hold out his hand, a broad smile on his face.

"I'd love to."

Taking his hand, he found a place in the middle and took her in his arms, guiding her through a two-step. *At least it was a step away from Mitch*, she thought as he led her around the floor, not noticing the brooding figure a few feet away.

Mitch leaned against a wood column in a darkened corner, watching Dana move across the room. He knew the cowboy who held her, and grimaced as she looked into the man's eyes, laughing at something he'd said. Mitch took a sip of whiskey, cursing himself for not being the one with her tonight. It had been his own doing, a result of his own experiences. He had no desire to go through what his father had, or relive the same betrayal he'd experienced with his college girlfriend. All the same, he couldn't get the feel of Dana off his skin or the look in her eyes when he held her in his arms.

He tossed back the rest of his drink and slammed the glass on the bar as he stormed out, vowing to purge Dana and the memories from his mind.

******

Dana tossed the last of the personal belongings she'd brought into her rolling bag and glanced around. Her computer case, jacket, and purse lay on a chair by the door. She'd stripped the bed, piling the towels on top of the sheets in the spot Sam had indicated the night before, and now waited for the cab to the airport.

As if on cue, a car pulled up the drive and stopped out front. She'd yet to hear any sounds from Mitch's room down the hall. For all she knew, he'd spent the night somewhere else. The thought brought a stabbing sensation to her heart, which she pushed aside as she grabbed her bags and slipped out the front door.

"The airport, ma'am?" the driver confirmed as he lifted her luggage into the trunk and opened her door.

"Yes, please." She focused on her hands clasped tight in her lap, deciding not to look over her shoulder as the ranch house disappeared behind her. Instead, she distracted herself by thinking through the list of items still left to do. It seemed to take no time at all to reach the airport and get her boarding pass. Purchasing a cup of coffee, she pulled out a book and waited, glancing at the clock every few minutes, wishing time would speed by rather than crawl at the pace of an elderly driver on the freeway.

"Flight 1210 to Fire Mountain is ready to board." The announcement startled her, even though she'd been expecting it. Within fifteen minutes she'd be in the air with no intention of ever wasting another minute reflecting on her night with Mitch.

Dana latched her seatbelt and stared out the window as the plane taxied across the runway. Brief moments passed before the massive engines fired in earnest, the pilot driving the plane forward as it lifted into the sky.

As they rose, she noted a lone figure perched on a motorcycle outside the tall cyclone fence. She pressed her face to the glass, trying to get a better look, and gasped, recognizing Mitch as he raised a hand before dropping it to his side.

******

Mitch pulled the collar of his coat tight around his neck to ward off the morning chill and shifted on the seat of his Harley. He'd followed the taxi at a discreet distance, turning onto a frontage road when the car continued to the departing planes section of the airport. Telling himself he wanted to make sure she got off safe, he woke early, grabbed a couple energy bars, and tinkered with his bike until Dana climbed inside the cab.

From his vantage point, he could see the passengers traverse the tarmac and climb the steps into the plane. He spotted Dana right off, carrying her computer with one hand, her other hand pulling the rolling bag behind her. Hefting it from the ground, she maneuvered the steps, stopping twice to regain her balance on the narrow, metal steps.

Berating himself once more for how he'd acted, Mitch cussed under his breath, keeping his eyes focused on the plane as it moved down the runway and halted, waiting its turn to take off. Never had he felt the loss of a woman the way he did Dana. One night with her and his whole world had shifted, and might never be righted.

Continuing to watch, he lifted his hand in farewell as the plane took off, climbing into a clear morning sky, making a wide turn and disappearing south.

******

Kansas City, Missouri

"Thanks for flying up here to meet with the committee, Gage." Matt walked alongside him toward the parking lot as the bright summer sun warmed the asphalt, creating waves of heat that fanned their faces.

"Are you kidding? I was looking for an excuse to get out of the Houston office, if just for a couple days. Don't know what inspired me to take on a desk job after all the years in rodeo." Gage laid his hat in the backseat of Matt's truck, then climbed into the passenger seat.

"For the same reason I'm traveling thousands of miles a year trying to secure stock contracts. Our bodies failed us and we have to eat." Matt's grin didn't quite reach his eyes. He'd found success with Double Ace Bucking Stock, as did Gage, and at least for now planned to stick with them.

After his meeting with Ivan Santiago, he'd spent several days at the company's stockyards near Houston.

For a new player in the stock contracting business, Double Ace had grown at a rapid pace with new contracts being signed at an average of one a week. Their size allowed them to fulfill most contracts with their own stock without bringing in partners. It wouldn't be long until that changed and they'd have to line-up sub-contractors if they wanted to continue to grow.

"You're right. Double Ace isn't as exciting as competing, but it's a good living and we get to stay close to what we love." Gage pulled out his phone and scrolled through messages, sending a few quick texts before sliding it back in his pocket. "Do you think you'll stick around a while?"

The two had been friends in the rodeo circuit before Gage left to take a job as the vice president in charge of fulfilling the contracts Double Ace won. He'd been the one to put Ivan in touch with Matt when it became obvious he could no longer compete.

"No reason not to. The money's good, I work with rodeo people, and get to travel. The difference is this time I'm not hauling all my gear behind a truck." Matt turned toward the highway leading to the airport. He checked his watch—still plenty of time before Gage's flight left for Houston to stop for lunch.

"I hear you, man. Plus we work for a company committed to being the biggest contractor in the country with what seems to be an unlimited amount of money."

"Have you been able to find out any more about the investors? Seems to me they stay pretty much in the background." Matt pulled into a barbeque place he'd heard about and cut the engine. The dinner with Ivan hadn't proven any more fruitful than their meeting.

"Not much. Two old cowboys who used to rodeo plus a consortium of investors from Mexico, but you already know all that. What I learned last week is while Ivan isn't an investor, his family is. The Santiago's are big landowners, here and in Mexico, plus they're into oil, telecommunications, cattle, and I don't know what else."

Taking a table near the front, they ordered, then drank their beers while they waited.

"What about the other Mexican investors?" Matt asked.

"Nothing that tells us much. The Santiago family is the primary partner, with the Castanedas and Zamoras holding minority ownership. I can't find much on either one of those families. The truth is, both are common names and I don't know which ones are the investors."

Digging into their plates of barbecued ribs, they ate in silence for long minutes, lost in their own thoughts and the delicious food. Not until the waitress brought a second round of beers did Gage continue.

"I'd like you to fly into Houston next week. I have a meeting with a company who supplies bucking stock."

"What do they want?" Matt asked.

"The usual, to get on our list for sub-contracting needs."

Matt knew a big part of being successful in the contracting business centered on partnering with other companies. Whether they ended up working with them or not, it was always a good investment of time to meet with them.

"Let me know when and I'll be there."

Chapter Twelve

Fire Mountain

"It's good to have you back, Dana."

"Thanks, Heath. I'm glad to be back and ready to put all the ideas we came up with into place. Cam and Mitch provided good input." She thought of the two, both capable and smart, yet so different in their approach and temperament.

"No issues getting approvals from them?"

"All I'll say is they both ended up signing off."

"I understand. I'll look forward to the meeting on Monday to review the progress." Heath disappeared into his office.

Dana returned to the office Friday afternoon after her plane landed, staying long enough to check messages and take a brief meeting with Amber before going home. She'd been gone almost two weeks, yet it felt much longer.

Unpacking and doing laundry didn't take much time, at least not as long as she'd hoped. At seven o'clock she poured a glass of water with lemon, picked up a book she hadn't finished, and curled up on the sofa. Reading the same two pages three times, she finally tossed the book aside and let her mind do what it wanted—think about Mitch.

Throughout the flight, the image of Mitch on his

motorcycle, hand in the air, stayed with her. Without a doubt, she believed the lone figure could be no one else. He'd followed her to the airport and waited for her plane to take off. But why? He got what he wanted. One night with her, then a speedy departure. *Well, I always aim to please*, she thought, feeling a slight bitter taste in her mouth.

At least she'd finished what Heath sent her to do and now they could move forward with updating the marketing plans for both MacLaren Rodeo and RTC. Within a month they'd launch the new initiatives. More ways to engage potential customers would be added in time, but for now, she felt a sense of accomplishment at the progress.

Hearing her phone ring, she glanced around, remembering it sat on the kitchen counter. She jumped off the sofa and grabbed it, noting the caller ID showed Amber, and experienced an immediate sense of disappointment. Whether Dana wanted to admit it or not, she'd hoped it might be Mitch.

"You want some company?" Amber asked.

"Sure, but where's Eric?"

"He and Kade took off on their bikes for an overnight campout at the national park. Brooke is out of town until tomorrow, and as you know, I got back a day early from my trip to Austin. They'd already made plans, so I told Eric to take off. I'll bring a bottle of wine with me. Have you eaten?"

"I have, but if you're driving by the dessert place, feel

free to stop."

"So it's like that, is it?" Amber asked.

"What do you mean?"

"Dessert is comfort food to you, something you eat when you're down—"

"Or happy."

"Whichever it is, I want to hear about it." Amber hung up, leaving Dana to stare at the phone and wonder how much she should say.

Telling her she'd had the most amazing one night stand with the president of RTC, who just happens to be a member of Amber's family, didn't seem appropriate. Grabbing a couple wine glasses, she decided the best approach would be to tell Amber they'd gone out, had a great time, but she doubted it would ever go anywhere. With luck, Amber would buy it.

******

Crooked Tree

"That's good news, Lizzie. When do you move?" Mitch cradled the phone between his ear and shoulder as he finished making a sandwich. Up since dawn, he decided to take a Saturday off, working outside of his own house before taking a trail ride to the back pastures.

"The job starts in a couple weeks, enough time for me to find a place in Missoula and get settled. How about celebrating with me tonight? Drinks, dinner, whatever."

Mitch listened with little enthusiasm. The drinks and dinner sounded good, the whatever, not so much. The thought of a woman besides Dana in his bed held little appeal. For the hundredth time he wondered how one night with her had made such a strong impact, changing his thoughts about how he spent his free time, and with whom. Even Lizzie's beautiful face and bountiful body held no appeal.

"Drinks and dinner for sure. My treat."

"All right, if that's all you want." Lizzie's disappointment was clear.

"How about Whiskey Dan's at seven?" Maybe after a few drinks, he'd warm up to the idea of taking her to bed. After all, he'd ruined any chance of being with Dana again. He might as well move on.

"Perfect. See you then."

Finishing his sandwich, he changed into the clothes he wore when working in his shop. He'd planned to show Dana his woodshop and studio before they left the other morning, a place reserved for family and close friends. It hadn't worked out.

The wood working area in the front had been set up similar to his father's workshop. Opening the door between the shop and artist studio never failed to impress visitors. Floor to ceiling glass highlighted a magnificent view across an open meadow toward majestic mountains in the distance. It felt as if he were looking at a painting each time he opened the door and gazed out.

Mitch worked in several mediums, preferring oils for

his landscapes. Closing the door, he turned back to his wood projects, deciding to focus on the table he'd started when he returned from Fire Mountain. He'd designed it for a particular person. Now, it might go to someone else or find a place in his house. Made of walnut, burls, and koa, it had been designed for use in a bedroom or maybe an office. A hidden drawer had been built into the back, requiring nothing more than a touch to open. Inside, a pad with numbers allowed access to the built-in box. He'd built it more for fun than as an actual place to hide anything of value as the entire table could be lifted and taken from the house with little effort.

At five-thirty he put away his tools, locked the shop, and headed for the house, stopping at the cloud of dust coming up the drive. As the truck neared, he recognized Sean behind the wheel.

"What brings you out here on a Saturday evening? I thought you had a date?" Mitch brushed dust from his pants as he strolled toward the truck.

Sean climbed out of the cab, tossing his keys on the seat before closing the door.

"I do, but Jeanie Naylor called while on her way to the rodeo in Wyoming. Seems two of her tires blew and she'll be delayed delivering the stock."

"Where is she?"

"Just over the border in Wyoming. Not that far."

"Does she need our help?"

"Says she has it covered, just wanted us to know. It's unusual to have two tires blow on those big rigs, though.

It's got me wondering." Sean followed Mitch into the house, accepting a beer before taking a seat in the family room.

"You think someone tampered with the tires?" Mitch tipped up the glass bottle, letting the cold liquid cool his throat.

"It's not impossible." Sean leaned forward, resting his arms on his knees, rolling the bottle between his hands. "Maybe I'm seeing goblins where none exist."

"Or maybe you aren't. Bulls have gone down sick, tested positive for steroids, and a few young bulls have gotten out. It's either an incredible run of bad luck or someone is targeting us."

"Do you think the broken fence is part of it?"

"Not really. I believe the calves got spooked and knocked it down, but I don't want to rule it out since we aren't sure. Which bulls does Jeanie have on this trip?"

Sean glanced at Mitch, knowing he wouldn't like the answer. "Absolute Devil."

Mitch winced at the knowledge their most profitable bull sat on the side of a road while two tires were being replaced. "I thought we agreed to move him in a separate group with Wretched and Grave Tender."

"Yeah, about that—"

"Dammit, Sean. Wasn't Emilio's half-brother driving them out in a separate trailer with his cousin riding along?"

"That was the plan. The half-brother came down with food poisoning, so we had to load the three on Jeanie's trailer. I suppose Emilio and Fritz could've taken them, but the calves had gotten out the day before and I was still dealing with the fallout of the steroid tests." Sean walked to the laundry room just off the kitchen, tossing his empty bottle in the recycle tub. "Maybe I should ride out where Jeanie's truck is broken down and follow her the rest of the way."

Mitch dragged a hand down his face, not comfortable with having no one except Jeanie watching over bulls which accounted for close to twenty-five percent of their earnings.

"Why don't you and I go? It's been a long time since we've been on a run together."

Sean studied him, wondering if the idea was a passing thought Mitch would kick to the side of the road upon further reflection, or a valid suggestion.

"As much as I'd like to, we both know we're needed here right now. Why don't we get Rhett to ride out with one of the men?"

Mitch wanted to argue, but Sean's idea had merit. They needed to stick around, handle any other fires that came their way. Each already had plans to visit specific rodeos where they held the contracts in an attempt to solidify their relationship with the committees. Double Ace seemed to be closing in on them from all around, pushing until the normal profit had been reduced significantly in order to secure the business.

"All right. I'll call Rhett, then Emilio, let him know I want Fritz to go with Rhett. You get in touch with Jeanie and have her stay put until Rhett and Fritz arrive." Mitch glanced at his watch, grimacing at the time. He'd be late meeting Lizzie. Nothing he could do about it now, not with Absolute Devil sitting off a Wyoming road.

Grabbing his phone, he hit Rhett's speed dial number and waited, remembering Saturday nights when he was Rhett's age. He sure hoped his brother picked up.

******

Mitch pulled off his hat and stepped into the bar of Whiskey Dan's, scanning the tables.

"Over here."

He looked toward a corner, seeing Lizzie wave at him, looking as good as ever. She got up from her place in the booth as he approached, wrapping her arms around his neck and placing a wet kiss on his lips. He wrapped his arms around her waist, feeling the soft curves in all the right places. Tonight her assets didn't entice him as they had in the past. In fact, if possible, he'd have one drink, dinner, then head home, preferring the quiet of his home to Lizzie's bed. The knowledge bothered him more than he wished.

"Hmmm...I'm glad you're here." Her sultry voice, which normally sent waves of arousal through him, did nothing. She placed another kiss on his mouth and slid back into the booth, leaving him a place next to her.

He ordered drinks then turned toward her, trying to get comfortable in the small space she left him. "Tell me about your new job."

"They specialize in corporate and real estate law. I met one of the partners in a Missoula law firm a few weeks ago. He mentioned an opening for a legal assistant, so I sent him my résumé. I've driven there twice for interviews and got the offer on Tuesday, countered on Wednesday, and received a final offer on Thursday, which I accepted." She sipped her Manhattan, a satisfied look on her face.

"How long have you known the partner?" Mitch knew how Lizzie worked. He didn't fault her for it and admired the way she set a course and went after what she wanted.

"We met while you were in Arizona. He'd been meeting with a client in town and came out one night. We hooked up, and well...it went from there."

"Be careful, Lizzie."

She slid a hand through his arm. "What do you mean?"

"How well do you know this guy? Did you do any checking on the firm?"

"Of course I checked on the firm. They have a great reputation. As for him, I knew from the start it wouldn't be a long-term thing."

"Yeah? And why's that?" Mitch had known Lizzie since high school. She had few inhibitions, including no hesitancy at all about sleeping with married men. His mother had been the same way.

"Well..." she stammered.

"He's married."

She pulled her hand free, picked up her drink and

took a long swallow. "Look, I know your feelings about it, so don't lecture me, okay?"

"If you know my feelings, then you also know I don't give a damn. From my experience, most women have no difficulty sleeping with married men, or sleeping with other men if they're married. It's not my problem."

"Because you never plan to marry."

"That's right. I don't see the point." Mitch sat back as the waiter set their plates down, nodding when asked about added pepper. When they were alone, he picked up his glass, tilting it toward her. "Here's to a great opportunity, Lizzie. I hope it works out for you."

She accepted the toast, then set her glass down. "You know, we can still get together when I'm in town."

He looked at her, his eyes revealing nothing. "We'll see."

******

Fire Mountain

"You two have done a great job. What's the timeline for changes?" Jace sat opposite Rafe with Heath at the head of the table, their department heads taking the other seats. Today Dana joined them, presenting an update on the marketing changes for the stock contracting companies.

"Thanks, Jace. It didn't take as long as we anticipated

to get to this point. There is a question we have, though."
Amber glanced at Dana, who already knew what she'd be
asking.

"Go ahead," Heath said, glancing up from the meeting
agenda.

"Since we're making all the changes, and you're
looking at buying a company that provides stock for timed
events, why don't we move all of them under the
MacLaren Rodeo Company banner now instead of
dragging it out?"

"Rafe, why don't you give us your thoughts?" Heath
sat back, waiting for Rafe to enlighten them as to why he
objected to changing the RTC name. The three brothers
had already been through several heated discussions on
the potential change, and each time Rafe almost came out
of his seat at the concept.

Rafe sat forward, setting his arms on the table, and
folding his hands together. As soon as he arrived back in
Fire Mountain, he'd been put in charge of closing the deal
with a company in Texas that supplied stock for rodeo
timed events. Cam's Cold Creek operation did some of
this, but not to the Texas firm. Through his contacts, Cam
had identified the opportunity a few months before,
stepping back when Rafe joined his brothers. Once the
purchase finalized, Rafe would become the executive in
charge of MacLaren Rodeo Company with Cam, Mitch,
and the timed event president reporting to him.

"The deal with Western Rodeo Stock closes the end of
this week, which rounds out our ability to provide every

animal needed for a rodeo, plus the men and equipment included in the proposals." He looked at Heath, then Jace, his mouth curving up in a slight smile. "Reflecting on the pros and cons of bringing all three groups under one name, I've come to realize it's in our best interest to present a unified front. I think we should move forward with using MacLaren Rodeo Company."

"I'll be damned," Jace murmured, his eyes wide, catching a similar look on Heath's face.

Rafe continued, explaining the logistics of preparing proposals and questioning whether each group should still be identified in some way as providing specific stock.

"I believe it might muddy things up to delineate specific stock, such as MacLaren Rodeo Company, Bucking Bulls. From a marketing perspective, it would be best to show one name, ignoring specific stock." Amber thought a moment before continuing. "However, we might be able to add an image to identify specific stock."

"I agree with Amber," Dana said. "Consistent branding is important for tying the companies together."

"How does this affect Cam, Mitch, and the president of the new company? Will there be one president or continue the way they are?" Eric normally stayed out of discussions of the stock companies, focusing on real estate acquisition and development, but how the changes played out could have a major impact on company revenues.

"Rafe will head the new division, while the presidents will continue in their current roles and report to him. We're in the process of setting up a meeting of everyone next week to discuss the change and other issues. We hope to have answers by the end of the quarter." Heath checked his watch, then looked to Amber and Dana. "Go ahead with MacLaren Rodeo Company, but I want to see your ideas on how we can identify each group by images or location. I want to have options to show Cam and Mitch."

Dana nodded, although her stomach did a summersault. Mitch would be coming to town sooner than anticipated. Since coming home, she'd done everything possible to stay busy, doing nothing to remind her of their night together.

Mitch would encounter a different Dana when he came to Fire Mountain. A woman who wouldn't dwell on the mistake she'd made—and it had been her choice to stay after his warning. Given the way they parted, she doubted he hoped for a repeat performance either. Maybe in time they'd be able to return to their good-natured sparring. At least she hoped they could.

Chapter Thirteen

Crooked Tree

"Thanks for jumping in and taking care of the delivery, Rhett." Mitch set a platter of burgers on the table. It had been a long Monday and the rest of the week promised no respite.

"Glad I could do it. Jeannie Naylor's an interesting woman."

"That she is." Sean laid a patty between two buns.

Mitch extended a fork to grab a burger when his phone rang. Groaning, he pulled it from his pocket as he stood and walked from the room.

"Mitch, it's Heath. We need you to fly down here for meetings on Wednesday. We're going to be discussing the newest acquisition and get thoughts from you and Cam on how to best integrate the company."

"Sure, Heath. Can you give me any information?"

"It's a company Cam learned about. They're located in Texas and supply stock for timed events. Rafe's been in charge of closing the deal and now we need to figure the best way to move forward. Count on a full day of meetings, maybe two. I'll send the company jet for you and have the pilot pick up Cam on the way back."

"Send me the details and I'll be ready." They hung up, Mitch's mind already jumping to Dana and the thought of seeing her again. Working in his woodshop kept his mind off her to some degree, but her image always seemed to find a way to break through his defenses and capture his mind. He'd lain awake each night, replaying their night together, still feeling her fingers running over his body. Even now his body tightened on the memory, frustrating him. He'd always been able to walk away from any woman and not look back. Relationships held no appeal to him, yet with Dana, he wanted more than casual sex.

"Who was it, Mitch?" Skye took another healthy bite of her burger.

"Heath. I need to attend meetings in Fire Mountain on Wednesday. Sean, are you able to handle things while I'm gone?"

"No problem. I don't travel until the following week. What about you, Skye?"

"I fly out Tuesday night to meet Cassie in Houston for the meeting with Double Ace. The return flight isn't until Thursday. Should I change it?"

"No need. Besides, it's important to get this first meeting out of the way, see if we can work out some type of partnership." Mitch took his first bite of food, letting the juice run down his fingers. Perfect.

"You'll get to see Dana again." Rhett concentrated on his food, not seeing Mitch's reaction.

"I'm going there for business, nothing more," he ground out.

"You'll be in the same building and you're going to ignore her?" Rhett's incredulous tone angered Mitch further.

"I don't know where your thoughts are going, but mine are clear. We went to dinner, had a good time, will continue to work together, but that's it. You understand me?"

Rhett blinked a couple times, noticing the hard set of Mitch's face. "Sure, Mitch. Whatever you say."

"Good. Now drop it." He stuffed the last bite in his mouth and took his plate to the sink, washing it before storming from the room without another word.

"What'd I say?" Rhett looked at Skye, then Sean, having no clue of the emotions he'd set off inside his brother.

"Nothing, Rhett. Just ignore him. But I would advise not mentioning Dana again, at least until he brings her up." Skye shadowed Mitch's actions, washing her dishes and putting them away.

Sean didn't contribute to the conversation, his attention wholly focused on Mitch's retreating back. He'd watched women come and go in his brother's life, most lasting no more than a night or two. Not once had Mitch ever reacted about one the way he did tonight. His usual response was indifference, never pushing back or becoming angry. He may not know his strong denial served to strengthen Sean and Skye's belief he cared about Dana more than he wanted anyone to know—perhaps even himself.

******

"Please, have a seat and I'll let Gage know you're here." The receptionist indicated chairs lined against a wall in a separate alcove adjacent to the lobby. The chairs faced a bank of windows with a view to a beautiful garden filled with indigenous plants.

"I haven't had a chance to ask how you like your new job." Skye straightened her skirt as she spoke. Other than her visit to MacLaren Enterprise headquarters in Fire Mountain, she'd never seen a stock contractor office so well designed. Artwork adorned the walls, and not just framed rodeo pictures. These were done in pastels, oils, watercolors, and acrylics. She'd love to bring Mitch here, have him see the beautiful art. It was too bad he never let anyone enjoy his talent outside of family and a few friends.

"I love it, although the time has gone fast. They're right in saying a college degree is more of a rite of passage as it bears little resemblance to what transpires in real life. I work with Cam every day and am doing more of the proposal drafts. I've also started meeting with rodeo committees, although I accompany Cam. He tells me it won't be long and he'll cut me loose." Cassie's smile lit her face. "How's it going at RTC?"

"Interesting." Skye didn't know how much she should share and decided on discretion until they were in a place where their voices didn't carry.

"What do you mean?"

"We've had a few setbacks that I'll explain to you at

dinner tonight." She tilted her head toward the receptionist, knowing Cassie would get the message.

"Got it."

"It will be about five more minutes, ladies. Gage apologizes for the delay."

"That's fine," Cassie responded, turning back to Skye. "How did Dana and Mitch get along?"

"He approved all her work, if that's what you mean."

"Not exactly. I'm more curious as to how they worked together. Dana seemed a little anxious about it before she left Cold Creek."

Skye didn't have a chance to answer as the door opened. She peered around the alcove wall to see a tall man dressed in typical cowboy clothes with features she'd consider rugged and strikingly handsome. Removing his hat, he walked toward the reception desk. Skye elbowed Cassie, who had been absorbed in checking phone messages, and inclined her head.

"Well, good morning," the receptionist greeted him. "Gage said you'd be in today."

"I flew in early for a meeting he asked me to attend. Do you know if he's ready?"

Cassie's heart rate skyrocketed at the sound of the familiar voice. Shifting in her seat, she turned to get a better look at him, taking in a gulp of air as her hands fisted in her lap.

"Not quite. The women over there will be in the meeting also."

Matt turned and smiled at Skye before he saw the

woman next to her. He couldn't move or speak as the room tilted around him. Gaining his composure, he took a few steps forward, close enough to confirm who stared back at him.

"Hello, Cass."

Cassie's throat worked, although she couldn't seem to form any words. He looked good—too good after all this time. Older with a few more wrinkles around his eyes and mouth. Tanned skin set off his golden brown eyes and deep auburn hair—sun bleached from being outside. She let her gaze wander over him, still not able to form a coherent thought or utter a word.

"Hi. I'm Skye MacLaren, and you are?" Skye stood, holding out her hand while drawing Matt's attention away from Cassie. She knew a little of the history from what Dana had shared and wanted to do whatever she could to ease Cassie's obvious distress.

Matt tore his gaze from Cassie, letting it move to Skye as he clasped her hand. "Matt Garner. I work for Double Ace. You're a MacLaren?"

"I am. Rafe MacLaren is my father. He, Jace, and Heath are brothers. Do you know the MacLarens?" Skye glanced down at Cassie, seeing her push from the chair to stand.

"Yes. I mean...we all grew up together in Fire Mountain, but I never heard of another brother."

Skye didn't doubt it. "Ah, then that's how you know Cassie."

"Yes, we...uh..." Matt's voice trailed off as he shifted

167

toward Cassie, seeing her jaw work, sparks flying from her eyes, her face set. "It's good to see you, Cassie. You're looking real—"

He didn't get the word out before a fist slammed into this face.

"Shit, Cassie." He held up one hand in defense while the other grabbed his nose as blood began to drip on the hardwood floor.

"You're a son of a bitch, Matthew Garner." She spat the words out, then rubbed her bruised knuckles, feeling better already.

He looked at her through the pain of what he guessed would be another broken nose. "Dammit, Cass. Don't you think I already know that?"

"What the hell..."

They turned to see another man enter from the hall. He looked at Cassie, who still rubbed her hand, then at Matt's face, his brows drawing together. "Are you all right, Matt?"

"Yeah, fine." Matt accepted tissues the receptionist offered, holding them to his nose. "Gage, this is Skye MacLaren," he murmured, nodding toward Skye who held out her hand.

"Hello, Gage."

"And who is this?" Gage narrowed his eyes on Cassie, whose anger still simmered.

"I'm Cassie MacLaren," she answered, never moving her gaze from Matt.

"And I'm guessing you and Matt have met before."

She crossed her arms and faced Gage, her hard stare locking with his.

"We have a long history, one I'm certain Matt will be more than happy to share with you." She picked up her purse, slinging it over her shoulder. "Are you ready for us now?"

******

Fire Mountain

"Dana's going to provide updates on the websites." Amber looked toward the far end of the table where Dana waited for her part of the presentation.

She hadn't planned to attend the meeting, figuring Amber would provide the marketing information to the executive group. Slipping into the conference room a few minutes after they'd taken a break, she spotted two empty seats. One at the end closest to her and the other next to Mitch. Seeing him nod his head toward the chair next to him, she smiled but shook her head, preferring to keep her distance.

He'd left her a message before the first session that morning, asking if she'd have time for lunch. She'd waited until the meeting began before texting him that she had other plans. He'd replied, asking about dinner. Again, she declined. As soon as her part of the presentation ended, she'd leave.

"Dana, would you mind holding up a minute while

Eric gives us an update on the Idaho project? He has a plane to catch."

"Of course not, Heath." The smooth, professional reply hid her frustration at not being able to get her part over with and disappear.

Eric's update took a mere fifteen minutes, yet it was long enough for Dana to calm her jitters. She'd made numerous presentations in her career, never feeling as on-edge as today. The difference between those meetings and this one was Mitch, and once again she chastised herself for letting him claim even a small piece of her heart.

"Thanks for letting me cut in on your time, Dana." Eric picked up his folders, said his goodbyes and left, leaving Dana to take his place.

She fired up her computer, pulling up a presentation page with three logos. Heath already let her know he'd spoken to Cam, Mitch, and the president of their newest acquisition, and all knew of the decision to transition them under the MacLaren Rodeo Company brand. At least she didn't have to fight that battle.

It took just a few minutes to review the updated websites which included the MRC logo. The difference between each website lay in the use of an image behind the logo—a bucking bull, saddle bronc, or steer roping. After answering a few questions, she finished, packing up her material and started for the door. As she turned the handle, the sounds of a groan and a chair tipping over had her swinging around to see Rafe hunched over and clutching his chest.

"Call 9-1-1." Heath's booming voice shook the room as he, Mitch, and Jace huddled around Rafe.

Dana snatched the phone from the table and dialed, explaining to the operator while she watched Rafe's face contort, fear and pain showing in his eyes as the others supported him so he wouldn't topple over.

"You need to sit down, Rafe." Jace righted the chair while Heath and Mitch guided him to it. Minutes dragged by while he struggled for breath and continued to clutch his chest until the door burst open and a crew of four paramedics went to work.

Dana stood to the side, her gaze shifting from Rafe to Mitch. He'd stepped back to allow the medics access, but hovered close, watching as they stabilized his father, lifted him onto a stretcher, and left for the waiting ambulance.

Mitch and the others followed as they loaded Rafe.

"Do you want to ride with him?" one of the paramedics asked Mitch, who wasted no time climbing inside before the doors closed and they drove out of the parking lot.

"I'm going to the hospital. Do you want to ride with me?"

Dana pulled her gaze from the retreating ambulance to Amber. "I'd better take my car. Mitch will need a ride at some point and at least I can leave him my Jeep."

They followed several cars out of the drive, including Heath, Jace, and Cam, forming a procession all the way to the visitor parking at the hospital. By the time they found seats in the waiting area, Mitch appeared from the emergency hallway, taking slow, lumbered steps toward them. Heath and Jace stood, talking to him in low voices, nodding before Mitch took a seat, covering his face with both hands.

Not five minutes later, a doctor Heath and Jace recognized walked up to Mitch, who stood, his face intent on what the doctor was saying. Motioning toward another door, the doctor left, Mitch following behind while Heath signaled to the others.

"They're moving Rafe to the cardio center to do an angiogram. There's a waiting room there which is less hectic."

One other family waited in the waiting area outside the cardiology surgery section. Everyone took a seat except Mitch, who paced back and forth, every once in a while glancing up at the patient progress screen mounted to the wall.

Dana watched until she couldn't sit still any longer and stepped into the hall. A sign mounted over a door a few yards away announced coffee and snacks were available inside. Inserting her money, she selected a black coffee, remembering how Mitch liked to drink it and returned to the waiting area.

"I thought this might help."

Mitch stared down at her without recognition, as if seeing her for the first time. Dragging a hand over his face, he took a breath and reached out to take the cup.

"Thanks."

"I know you don't have any answers, but is there

anything I can do to help while we wait?"

He didn't respond right away, taking a sip of the steaming coffee then glancing around the room.

"Would you mind calling Sean?"

"Of course. I'll do it right now." Dana placed a hand on his arm and squeezed. Even the stress of the situation didn't diminish the jolt she experienced at the brief touch. The look on his face told her he felt it, too. "I...um...need to get my phone."

The conversation took little time, with Sean saying he'd contact Skye and Rhett, then be on the first plane to Fire Mountain. The last words he said before hanging up confused her.

"Stay with him, Dana. He needs someone he feels close to."

"I'll stay as long as he needs me."

Chapter Fourteen

Houston

"All I want to know is, did it feel good?" Skye asked, nursing a frozen margarita.

"Great. If my knuckles hadn't stung so much I would've hit him again." The corners of Cassie's mouth tilted upward, although her eyes didn't sparkle as Skye expected.

"Did you see the look on his face when he saw your fist come at him?"

"You know, I don't remember much besides the strong desire to vent my anger. From the time he walked in until I hit him is pretty much a blur." She sipped her drink, shaking her head at the impulsive move, then glancing at Skye. "I don't know how what I did will affect Gage's decision about working together."

"He deserved it, so right now I don't care much one way or the other. RTC and MacLaren Rodeo will continue to do fine with or without Gage Templeton's approval."

"Thanks, Skye. I feel bad for Cam, though. I know he counted on me to impress Gage."

Skye laughed, placing a hand on Cassie's arm. "There's no doubt you impressed the man. I doubt he'll ever forget you." She started to flag the waitress for another drink when her phone rang.

"Hi, Sean. Are you checking up on us?" A mischievous smile crossed her face before it vanished in a flash. "Where is he?" She glanced at Cassie, her face turning an almost pasty white as she listened to Sean. "Yes. I'll catch the first plane I can." Skye lowered the phone to her lap in almost slow motion, her face showing no signs of returning to its previous glow.

"What is it?"

"It's Pop. He's had a heart attack and is in surgery at the hospital in Fire Mountain." She rose, slinging her purse over her shoulder. "I have to leave."

"Come on. I'll get you to the airport." Cassie hurried alongside Skye, deciding not to put her on a plane but accompany her home. Making a brief stop at the hotel for their luggage, Cassie settled their tab and took off for the airport.

They were fortunate. The last plane had extra seats and within an hour they were in the air. By eleven o'clock they entered the waiting area filled with family members who'd refused to go home until they'd been allowed to see Rafe.

Cassie ran up to Heath, wrapping her arms around him. "How is he, Dad?"

"We're still waiting for word from the doctor."

"Where are Mitch and Sean?" Skye asked as Heath gave her a hug.

"Sean's outside on a phone call." Heath nodded toward the double glass doors. "Mitch and Dana are in the cafeteria. They should be coming back upstairs any time now."

She joined Sean outside while Cassie took a seat next to Heath.

"What happened?"

Heath explained Rafe's seizure during the meeting and results of the angiogram.

"No one knew, except his kids, that he had three stents as the result of a seizure a few years ago. His ex-wife doesn't even know about it, even though they were married at the time."

"How could that be possible?" Cassie couldn't imagine Heath keeping that from Annie.

Heath shrugged. "They're marriage had been going downhill a long time. She vacationed quite a bit, so it wasn't hard to keep it quiet." He picked up his lukewarm coffee and took a sip. "After performing the angiogram a few hours ago, the doctor recommended minimally invasive double bypass surgery instead of adding more stents. At first Rafe leaned toward the stents, then changed his mind."

"Is he in surgery now?"

"He is. The way I understand it, they're treating it as emergency surgery due to the amount of blockage." Heath glanced at his watch. "Shouldn't be too much longer."

Skye and Sean walked inside, taking seats next to Cassie and Heath at the same time Jace, Amber, Kade, and Brooke came into the waiting area carrying sacks of food.

"No sense everyone going hungry while we wait."

Amber placed her bags on a table. "Any word?"

"Nothing yet," Sean answered, waving off a sandwich Kade held out to him. "Thanks, but I'm going to wait."

The others nibbled at their food, hopeful a positive report would come to them soon.

******

"Here you are. There wasn't much choice at this time of night so I grabbed a turkey and a ham." Dana laid the sandwiches in front of Mitch and a salad at her place. "This must all come as a shock. He seems much too young to have heart issues."

They'd sat outside on the patio for a time, saying little until the air became too chilled and they returned to the cafeteria. Even though neither mentioned it, a tentative truce formed as the evening turned to night and everyone waited.

"This is his second time under the knife. The first time shocked all of us. Afterwards he changed his diet, exercised, even stopped his once or twice a week cigars. He seemed fine." Mitch unwrapped a sandwich and took a bite, chewing slowly.

"Stress?"

Mitch focused on the food in his hand, as if studying it would provide answers.

"No more than usual. A year ago, when Heath and Jace bought RTC, I'd have said yes. The last few months have been much better. He's had to deal with a lot of changes."

"I guess learning you have another son would have been a big one" Dana picked at her salad, pushing it around her plate.

"It was, but he handled it pretty well, given the circumstances. Pop's always had a hard time with change."

"Like father, like son?" she joked, seeing a slight smile touch Mitch's mouth before her expression grew serious. "Is there any reason to call your mother?"

He'd been asking himself the same question all evening. His mother and Rafe hadn't gotten along in years. Arguments followed by silence increased over time. After Rafe learned of the affair, the divorce seemed a formality.

"You may have heard my mother had a long affair with some guy she met on one of her frequent trips. She never liked the ranch, RTC, or being stuck in what she considered a hick town lacking any social life, so she created her own fantasy life with this other man."

"How did you learn about it?"

"I walked in on her and the son of a bitch," he snorted, seeing Dana's eyes widen. "I'd just turned fourteen, thought I knew everything, even though I acted like a punk much of the time. Mother said she and friends were going shopping, so I ditched school, believing no one would be home. I heard noises from her room and opened the door to see...well, you can figure it out."

"I can't imagine," Dana whispered, sensing some of

the pain Mitch must've felt at the betrayal to his father.

"Believe me, it's a sight you never want to witness. Anyway, Mother panicked. Begged me not to say anything to Pop. I was big for my age and confronted the guy, told him to get the hell off our property and never come back." He blew out a breath, not sure why sharing one of the most painful parts of his life with Dana felt right. "I couldn't look at or speak with my mother for months."

"Did you tell Rafe about it?" She pushed her salad away as her hunger vanished.

"No, at least not that time."

"You mean it happened again?"

"She couldn't stay away from the guy. He never stepped foot in our house again, but I guess they continued to meet whenever they could. I worked at RTC during high school, doing whatever they needed, cleaning corrals, helping with the bulls, running errands. One day during my senior year Pop asked me to take a file to his attorney in town. I drove past this no-tell motel type of place and whose car sat parked in front of one of the rooms? Mother's," he bit out. After all this time he still felt anger at what she did to his father. "I parked and pounded on the door. When it opened, the same guy stood there, half dressed, my mother behind him on the bed with sheets wrapped around her..." his voice trailed off at the memory.

They sat in silence a few minutes until Mitch spoke again.

"I couldn't form a sentence, just stared at her, then

turned and left." He shook his head, his lips forming a thin line. "I'd stopped at a burger place on the way into town and finished it before spotting her car. I lost it all about a quarter mile past the motel." He looked at Dana. She could still see the pain after all these years. "Seventeen-years-old and I had no clue what to do."

"He found out, though."

"I gave her a choice—either she told him or I would. She told him. Promised it would never happen again, which I knew was crap. She just didn't want to go through the mess of a divorce. Mom stuck around until Skye left for college, then moved to California. No one filed for a long time, then Pop finally decided to get an attorney." He pushed away from the table, stood, and stretched his arms above his head. "Guess we should head back upstairs."

She followed him to the elevator, placing a hand on his arm. "You know, anytime you want to talk—about anything..."

He stared down at her, a look she couldn't quite decipher in his eyes before a small grin appeared.

"Who would've thought Dana Ballard would be such a good listener?"

"Hey, I have a lot of skills I keep tucked away for use in emergencies. Text, phone, email—whatever works for you." They stepped into the elevator and punched the floor for cardio surgeries.

Mitch stilled, his voice dropping to a whisper as the door closed behind them. "Would that include talking over dinner?"

She felt the same rush of heat as with the first time he'd asked. Now she knew to keep her distance so he didn't burn her a second time.

"Dana?"

She swallowed, deciding there'd be no repeat of what happened before. "*Dinner* would be nice." She flashed him a warm smile as the elevator dinged, signaling their floor.

******

"Can't you get me out of here any sooner?" Rafe's mood had deteriorated since the operation. Not from the surgery, which had been a success. He hated hospitals. Being tested and probed, eating passable food, getting little or no sleep, and having doctors and nurses ask the same questions over and over, turned relief at his prognosis to frustration.

"Doc's going to check you out tomorrow morning. If he gives the okay, I'll get you out of here." Mitch picked up one of the plastic covered bowls, lifted the top and sniffed. "Hmmm..."

"Do you have any idea what that stuff is?" Rafe shifted on the bed, pushing the cord of the call button to the side.

"Not a clue." Mitch guessed it to be pudding, although he wouldn't swear to it.

"And that's a damn good reason why I'm not eating it." He grimaced, shifting again to find a more comfortable position.

"How's the patient?" Skye asked as she walked in, a

181

small bag in her hand.

"He'd be doing better if he were home," Rafe said, eyeing the bag. "What's in there?"

"Not much. A toasted bagel and chicken sandwich." She dangled it in front of him, snatching it away when he reached for it. "Half now and half later."

"Fine." Rafe grabbed the bag, opened the top, and sniffed in the aroma. "It's been three days since I've had edible food. Thanks, honey."

"Are you sure it's all right for him to have that?" Mitch watched him take an unrepentant bite.

"The doctor gave the approval before I left for the deli. Of course, I had him alone in the elevator and wouldn't let him out until I pleaded Pop's case. He relented when I reminded him he'd have to face Pop later today."

Dana could hear the laughter coming from Rafe's room as she walked up the hall. After learning the surgery had been a success, she'd stayed away, wanting to give Rafe's family time alone with him. She also wanted to keep a healthy distance between her and Mitch. Knocking, she pushed the door open and poked her head inside.

"Am I interrupting?"

"Not at all. Come on in." Skye moved to the other side of the bed, giving Dana room to stand next to Mitch, who stood and pulled his chair over, brushing her arm in the process.

"Have a seat. I've been sitting all morning." Instead of moving aside, Mitch stepped closer, crowding her without drawing any attention to his movements.

"You look much better than the last time I saw you." She smiled at Rafe, seeing his color had improved, at the same time ignoring her body's response to Mitch standing so close.

"Which would have been in the ambulance?" Rafe asked.

"Yep." She glanced around the large private room with a view toward the mountains. "Not that this isn't a great room, because it is, but when do you get to go home?"

"See, even Dana thinks I should be let loose." His grumbled response sounded more upbeat than when he'd complained to Mitch.

"The doctor will check his progress in the morning. If all looks good, the old man will be staying in his own bed tomorrow night." Mitch leaned past Dana to help Rafe change positions, hearing an intake of breath as his thigh brushed against hers.

"Old man, huh? You remember that when I best you at the next family rodeo."

"Family rodeo?" Dana had heard nothing of this event.

"Each year the family here in Fire Mountain holds a rodeo in the area in front of the ranch house. This year we've been invited." Skye looked at Dana, her brows rising. "You might be ready to compete in barrel racing this summer. Cassie's says you're a natural."

"What barrel racing?" Mitch's gaze narrowed on Dana.

She turned toward him, ignoring the hard face and set

183

jaw. "Cassie spent quite a bit of time teaching me when I was in Cold Creek. I'll never win a medal, but I can clear all three without knocking them down. No one would mistake my turns for being tight." Dana's eyes sparkled as she spoke.

"You've had, what, a couple lessons, and now you're thinking of going up against Cassie, Skye, and Amber, risking injury doing something you know little about?"

Setting fisted hands on her hips, she glared up at him. "If it's a family and friends event for fun, then I don't know why not. All anyone can do is laugh at me. You have a problem with it, big guy?"

Mitch held up his hands, palms out, realizing he'd already revealed too much. There'd been four women he cared about in his life—his mother, Skye, Sam, and his college sweetheart. Over the years the number had been reduced to his two sisters, and no matter how much he told himself they were grown, able to take care of themselves, he couldn't shake the worry something might happen. Confusion and conflicting feelings gripped him as he began to comprehend the same worry had transferred to Dana.

"No problem. Just stating my case."

"Good, because if I get an invitation, I'm going to give it a try."

Skye watched the two, knowing more went on between them than either wanted to admit. After Dana left Crooked Tree, Mitch began to snap out orders and became a general pain. It had been a relief to leave for Houston and let Sean, Sam, and Rhett deal with him. Although guarded, Mitch seemed more at ease with Dana around.

"I'd better get going so you can visit with Skye and Mitch. It's good to see you looking better, Rafe." Dana cast a look at Mitch, then turned to leave.

"Hold on a minute, Dana. I'll walk you out." Mitch followed her toward the hall. "Anything you want while I'm downstairs, Pop?"

"Whiskey?"

"You wish. I'll be right back." He kept pace alongside Dana, resting a hand on the small of her back, wanting the connection he'd missed since she'd left Montana. Mitch had no idea why he felt this strong pull to be near her. Since the betrayal of his college girlfriend, and their breakup, he'd avoided all entanglements, never allowing any woman to get close. Dana had broken through his defenses, and though he still didn't see a future, he wanted to find some way to keep her in his life.

"Thanks for coming downstairs." Dana turned toward him in the lobby, searching his face, for what, she didn't know. "You don't need to go outside."

"Where's your Jeep?" Ignoring the comment, he guided her toward the door.

"Rafe looks much better."

"Yeah."

"Has he been able to get up, walk around?"

"Yeah."

His one word responses began to grate on her. Why had he volunteered to walk her out if he wanted to ignore her?

"Will you be going straight back to Crooked Tree when he's released?"

"No."

Spotting the Jeep, he stopped at the driver's side door and glanced around.

"Is this all I'm going to get? One word—"

She didn't finish before he wrapped his arms around her, pulling her flush against him, his mouth capturing hers. Surprise turned to passion as she threaded her fingers through the hair at the back of his neck and held on. Nothing about the kiss was gentle. Heat surged through her as he lessened the pressure, then trailed soft kisses on the edges of her mouth, along her jaw, to the soft column of her neck.

Loud laughter had them pulling apart, each gasping for air as they looked around, spotting a family getting into their car.

Dana's mind rocked at the intensity of his assault, and she chided herself on letting him suck her in so easily. Taking a deep breath, she straightened her spine, and looked into eyes which had turned a deep, stormy gray.

"What are we doing, Mitch?"

Keeping his arms slack at his sides, he glanced away, deciding how to answer. He'd always been better with the truth, no matter how blunt.

"I want to keep seeing you."

"I see." She nodded in a slow movement. "I assume this means you want me in your bed."

"Of course."

"For how long?"

"I don't know."

She crossed her arms, leaning against the side of her car, her eyes narrowing. "And what happens when the desire wears off?"

Dragging a hand through his hair, he shifted from one foot to another. "We go our separate ways. Until then, we enjoy each other."

Catching her lower lip between her teeth, she bit down hard enough to stop herself from saying what first came to mind. He didn't need to know how she thought of him at the most inconvenient times, remembering every moment of their night together, and the way her heart raced whenever she saw him. He wouldn't care.

"So the deal is we have sex with no strings attached until it's no longer fun."

He winced at her definition, although it captured what he wanted. All the pleasure and none of the potential pain associated with a long-term relationship or commitment.

"Yes."

Dana sorted through her choices. She could back out now and avoid the pain when he decided the excitement had worn off. Jump in with both feet and relish every minute, knowing it wouldn't last. Or go along with the sex without strings, try to keep it light while hoping he might change his mind, perhaps grow to care for her the way she already did for him. The last held the most risk, but also the most promise. She'd lost before, picked up the pieces and moved on. Dana had no doubt she could do it again.

"All right, we'll do it your way. But don't come whining to me when you can't let me go."

"Oh, I'll be able to let you go."

"I'll take that bet." She smiled, running a finger down his shirt.

He studied her, his chest tightening at the thought she might be right.

"With some ground rules," she added.

"Ground rules?"

"First, no repercussions at work. You're a MacLaren with a secure place in the company. When it's over, if I choose to stay with the company, you won't try to push me out."

"Done."

"Second, no one knows we're friends with benefits. What we do will be between the two of us and no one else."

"All right."

"And third, we don't see others while we're together. If you want to be with someone else, tell me and I'll disappear like that." She snapped her fingers. "No drama, just gone. And I'll do the same. If I meet someone else, I'll let you know."

He considered the last rule. The thought of Dana with another man burned like a hot poker in his gut. Mitch pushed it aside, knowing he'd see her for a month or two, maybe three, then move on. At that point he wouldn't care who she saw.

"Agreed. Now, if you don't have plans, let me say goodnight to Pop and take you to dinner. I'll be right back."

Dana leaned against her Jeep, watching him walk through the sliding entry doors. He'd be in Crooked Tree most of the time, which meant she'd see little of him. Long distance relationships took work, and in her opinion, Mitch didn't have the stamina for something requiring effort when all he wanted was sex. Quick and easy is how she saw him.

Climbing inside, she rested her head against the seat and thought about their agreement. It sounded crazy, scary, and perhaps what she needed to shake up her non-existent love life. He wouldn't be in it for love, but Dana couldn't help herself from believing he cared about her more than he'd ever admit.

Chapter Fifteen

"You know, this is the first place you and I ate together." Dana scanned the menu, recalling when she and several of the MacLarens came here for supper not long after her arrival in Fire Mountain. It had become one of her favorite restaurants.

Mitch picked up his wine glass, remembering that night. He'd been attracted to her even then, but shied away, not wanting to get involved with anyone, least of all a smart-mouth woman who couldn't stop asking questions.

"I remember. You drove me crazy with your continual chatter. I thought you'd never stop talking." Swirling the wine, he watched the deep red liquid coat the sides of the glass before taking a sip.

"And all this time I thought that's what you liked best about me."

The grin she sent him lit her face—a face he wanted to cradle in both hands before devouring her luscious lips, then continue until he'd satisfied this incessant craving. Mitch thought of her taunting statement about not being able to let her go, knowing he would walk away at some point, no matter his feelings for her. The best solution would be to shut this down now so no one got hurt. His mind pulled him in one direction while his instincts demanded he continue on the current path. The tug of war created an internal conflict he had no idea how to resolve.

Dinner dragged on with him dropping further into one of his dark moods as he wrestled with the situation he created. Dana sensed the change and tried to pull him out of it with small talk about their horses, motorcycles, and trips she hoped to take. Nothing worked.

Mitch continued to sip his wine, finishing his dinner, and lifting his gaze to hers every few minutes. He sensed the tension increase between them and knew he had to clear the air. The entire situation—the deal they'd agreed to—bothered him. He didn't understand why a similar arrangement with Lizzie hadn't caused any of the doubts and recriminations he wrestled with now.

He sat back in the chair, his eyes searching hers, seeing nothing of the laughing, upbeat woman who'd hooked him months before with her humor and wit. Leaning forward, he settled the wine glass between his hands, rolling it one way then another.

"I need to know you're sure about this, Dana. Getting involved in something that has little chance of ending well."

Her eyes widened, signaling her surprise they were back to this after deciding to see each other. She suspected he'd changed his mind. Perhaps he realized dating someone within the company made no sense when numerous women, with no connection with the MacLaren companies, were more than willing to provide what he sought. Or he may have decided traveling back and forth created too much of a hassle. She crossed her arms, deciding to confront the comment head-on.

"I haven't changed my mind, but if you have, just say so. I'll head home, you'll go back to Montana, and it ends." She picked up the almost empty bottle of wine, topping off his glass then pouring the last of the wine into her own. "I'm a big girl, but if you don't believe you can handle it..." She let her words trail off as she took a swallow of wine, her tongue darting out to lick the remains from her lips.

Mitch didn't respond before tossing his napkin on the table, cursing silently as he signaled for the check. Standing to pull out her chair, he grasped Dana's elbow, escorted her to the car, then turned her toward him. His jawed worked as his stormy eyes darkened, then narrowed.

Dana ignored the turbulence in his stare, wrapped a hand behind his neck and pulled him down to within an inch of her mouth, then stopped.

"I want this, Mitch. If you don't, just say the word."

One moment she felt in control, the next, an arm encircled her, pulling her, almost violently, to him. He crushed his mouth to hers, coaxing her to open and sweeping his tongue inside. Holding tight, she clung to him, allowing herself to get lost in the moment without regard for who might venture past and see them.

Loosening his grip, he pulled back, resting his forehead against hers.

His hoarse whisper broke the silence. "Let's get out of here."

The ride to the cabin he used when in Fire Mountain dragged on, Dana sitting close, her hand on his thigh, squeezing.

"Keep doing that and you'll have me driving off the road." The huskiness in his voice warned of how close he was to losing control.

Her sultry pout accompanied the removal of her hand and an increase in distance between them. "We can't have that. Not when we're so close."

Shooting a quick glance at her, he saw her eyes twinkle in amusement. "I will get you for this."

He'd barely shut off the engine before both jumped from the car, almost running to the door as he fumbled with the key. Shoving the door open, he followed her in, closing it an instant before she launched herself at him, both frantic to get back to what they'd started.

Soft moans and a trail of clothes marked their path to the bedroom where he swung her into his arms, stepped inside, and kicked the door closed.

******

A ringing in the distance forced Mitch's eyes open. A comforting warmth surrounded him, and he glanced down to see Dana sprawled across his chest, her leg over his thighs. He smoothed a hand down her silken red hair, which flowed across her back, then breathed in the scent of vanilla and fresh flowers as his hand moved up and down her back.

The phone ringing again stopped his movement. Groaning, he slipped out from under Dana, followed the sound into the living room, and grinned, spotting the piles of clothing strewn around the floor. He pulled the phone out of his pants.

"Hello."

"Mitch?"

"Yeah, who is this?" He knew his voice sounded harsh, but the call interrupted what he'd hope would be another round of incredible sex.

"Emilio. Sorry to bother you so early, Mitch."

"What's the problem?" He wanted Emilio to get right to the point so he could slip back into bed.

"It's Absolute Devil. He tested positive for steroids."

The announcement broke Mitch's morning tranquility. "Say that again." He paced toward the front window, trying to control the anger pulsing through him.

"Doc Wheaton tested him and it came back positive. He's scheduled to go out tomorrow for a rodeo in Idaho. What do you want to do?"

He scrubbed a hand down his face. "Substitute another bull. We can't send him out until he's clean. What about Wretched and Grave Tender?"

"Both clean. Look, Mitch. I asked the doc to do the test twice on Absolute. Both came back positive. There's no doubt he's been injected with steroids, but I can't figure out who got to him. I've had men posted all day and night for weeks."

"At least you caught it before transporting him to

Idaho. We keep this within the company, Emilio, until we figure out what's going on." Mitch heard the sound of footsteps behind him, then felt arms wrap around his back, hands clasping at his waist. Placing a hand over Dana's, he squeezed, jolted by how much he liked the comforting feel of her. "I need to check on Rafe as the doctor's supposed to release him today. I'll fly back as soon as I get him settled." Mitch hung up, his mind reeling at all that had happened.

"What's going on?" Dana's sleepy voice and warm skin had him aching to take her back to bed.

Mitch turned around, wrapped his arms around her, snuggling her into his body.

"Another bull tested positive for steroids." He rested his chin on the top of her head. "At least we found out before transporting him to a rodeo."

She glanced up, her eyes full of concern. "What will you do?"

"We have to find out who's getting to our animals. I hate to think it, but someone who works for us must be involved. Even if it's an outsider calling the shots, they have to have a man inside working for them." He took a deep breath. "I need to get Pop settled, then fly back."

"I know. I'll take a shower and be ready to go." She placed a kiss on his chest then turned toward the bathroom, picking her clothes off the floor as she went.

He watched her go, shaking off the feeling of loss. With the significant problems at RTC, he had no time for anything other than hooking up when convenient.

Besides, Dana had made herself available and was certainly willing. Reminding himself it was just sex, with no commitments, he grabbed his clothes and followed her.

******

"Let me go back. You stay here a few more days with Pop." Sean had received a similar call from Fritz, telling him about Absolute Devil's test. They both knew if word of this got out, it would add to the already mounting doubts about the company.

"No. I'm the one who needs to be there." Mitch pulled Rafe's pants and shirt out of a bag and laid them on the hospital bed. "You stay with Pop until you're sure he's fine."

"Dammit, don't talk about me like I'm not two feet away." Rafe pushed into a sitting position. "The doc's cleared me to go home. Drive me to Heath's, then both of you take off and let me get some rest."

"Sorry I'm late. Who knew they had traffic in Fire Mountain." Skye walked in carrying a tray with four cups of coffee. "I hope I got this right." She passed them out, her brows knitting together at the looks on the men's faces. "What's going on?"

Mitch explained about the test as well as he and Sean heading home.

"I'll stay a few more days then fly up," she offered.

"No. You will go home with your brothers. I'm not some damned invalid who can't take care of himself.

Besides, Annie's already arranged to have a nurse come by the house to check on me. Now, help me get my pants on."

By the time a nurse arrived with a wheelchair, Mitch had made arrangements for them to fly back to Crooked Tree that afternoon on the company jet. Following behind the nurse, he thought of Dana. They'd driven to her apartment, going inside long enough for him to draw her into his arms and say goodbye.

Mitch had no idea how long it would be before they'd see each other again. She accepted it, smiled, then waved as he drove off. He should've been thrilled at her behavior, how she'd let him go with no signs of regret at his departure. Intense sex with no strings. What any man would want. Then why did her indifference bother him so much?

******

Houston

"Sure seems they've experienced their share of problems." Gage Templeton hung up the phone, looking across the desk at Matt Garner, and shook his head at the bruising on his friend's face. "How's your nose?"

"Better. That woman can land a punch." Matt touched the side of his nose, wincing at the tenderness he still felt after almost a week. "Now I regret showing her how."

"You taught her to hit?" Gage laughed, remembering the scene in the lobby and Cassie's unrepentant attitude.

"Yeah. Guess what goes around comes around." He'd taken her to the gym several times, teaching her defensive moves for protection, never thinking they'd be turned on him. "And yes, RTC is getting hammered. Sick bulls, positive steroid tests, broken down big rig, and now Rafe MacLaren's heart attack."

News traveled fast in the stock contracting business and it didn't take long for his heart attack to hit the grapevine. Matt had called Cassie after he heard about Rafe, but she never returned his message. He didn't blame her. His selfish action years before had severed any chance of ever getting her back, or renewing a friendship with the MacLarens. Even though he had his reasons for leaving—and good ones from his perspective—he'd do anything to reverse his impulsive behavior. The loss of the MacLarens, and especially Cassie, had left a hole in his life that haunted him every day.

"Any chance someone may be after them, trying to sabotage their business?" Gage didn't believe in coincidences and the issues at RTC didn't smell right.

Matt fingered the brim of the hat resting in his lap. "Could be. Does it matter?"

"It does if Double Ace approves them for sub-contract work."

"True, and I'm glad you're still looking at them after what happened."

"Hey, all that's between you and Cassie MacLaren. Must have been a real shock to see you here, a part of Double Ace."

Matt lowered his head, not commenting. He'd been as stunned as Cassie.

"Regardless, both companies are solid with excellent reputations. We'd be foolish not to approve them, assuming the issues at RTC are resolved." Gage rubbed his chin with the knuckle of his index finger. "Why don't you make some calls, see if you can learn anything at all from your contacts and I'll do the same with mine? Something tells me it's sabotage and I don't want them looking to us. Best to see if we can find a connection, someone who holds a grudge or just wants them out of the competition."

"Sure. There are several people I can contact, but it's doubtful they'll know much." Matt pulled out his phone, scrolling through the names to identify people who might be willing to share what they've heard, if anything. "It could be a run of bad luck and nothing more."

"Maybe, but somehow I don't think so."

******

Crooked Tree

"Thanks, Doc. I'm glad you could come by to meet with us." Mitch stood and shook Gayle Wheaton's hand. She'd replaced the vet who retired a year before and seemed to be doing a real fine job. Slim and no more than five-feet-four-inches tall, he'd been surprised when Rafe had accepted her without comment. Tending big animals could be strenuous work. With her slight frame and five-foot-four height, Mitch had been skeptical.

"Anytime, Mitch." She glanced around the office, noticing the framed pictures and awards for civic work. "I've been up here just a couple times and never noticed all the plaques. Must feel good being so successful."

"It's not too different from any business. Lots of hard work and long hours."

"I suppose a lot of stock contractors don't make it. I mean, from what I've seen, the competition must be stiff." Gayle continued to look around, this time at the trophies and medals. "Did all of your family compete?"

He followed her gaze, a wan smile crossing his face. "In different events during high school and college. Samantha and Rhett still compete, but it's doubtful they'll continue on in the pro circuit."

"Because they'll come into the business?"

"If that's what they want. It's up to them." His phone vibrated in his pocket and he slid it out, seeing Dana's face and letting it go to voicemail. He'd sent her a text earlier, inviting her to fly up for the weekend.

"I'd better take off. Call me anytime."

He followed her to the second floor landing and watched as she took the first few steps to the lobby. "Thanks again, Doc."

Closing his office door behind him, he called Dana, a strange sense of anticipation passing over him.

"Hey...yes, I'm fine. The vet just left the office. She's coming by almost every day to make sure everything checks out... Good, you got my text... That's great. I'll make the arrangements and send you the flight information." He listened a minute before interrupting her. "No way in hell are you staying in a motel. You're staying with me and I don't care who sees you... Good. I'll see you Friday night."

Chapter Sixteen

Stepping into the air conditioned passenger area, Dana looked around trying to spot Mitch.

"Hey."

She turned to see him walk up and lean down to take her bag, not making any move to pull her into his arms or plant a kiss on her mouth. Following his lead, she kept her distance.

"Hi. Hope you didn't have to wait for me."

"Nope, the plane landed right on time. The truck's out that door." He nodded then followed her outside, loading her bag in the back seat. "I thought we'd grab dinner then go to my place."

"Sounds great. I'm famished."

Pulling into traffic, he turned down the radio before exiting onto a narrow country road. "Mexican okay for tonight?"

"Works for me." She placed a hand over her stomach, hoping to quell the butterflies that had plagued her since boarding the plane in Fire Mountain. Skirting Amber's questions about her weekend, she'd mentioned visiting friends out of town, and drove straight from the office to the airport. The excitement which ripped through her when his text arrived asking about flying up had stayed with her the rest of the week, along with the smile she couldn't contain.

They turned onto a narrow road with a sign pointing toward an old framed house in the distance. "Juan Diego's has been here since before I was born. Pop used to bring all of us here for special occasions. I didn't know it until a few months ago, but this is where he used to bring Kade's mother when they were dating."

"Does it still bother you?"

"You mean having an older brother, or my father loving another woman?"

"Both, I guess."

He parked and turned off the engine, then turned toward her. "It all happened before he ever met Mother, so no, the fact he loved someone else makes no difference to me. Kade took more getting used to, but I think we're good now."

"He's a good man, Mitch. You both are."

He fought a chuckle, not knowing if either of them were good men, but they tried. "C'mere." He reached over, wrapping a hand behind her neck and pulling her to him. "I can't wait any longer," he said as his mouth descended on hers.

Careful not to let it heat up too much, he kept his desire controlled, saving his hunger for later.

"Are you certain you're starving?" he whispered against her lips.

Dana pulled back, her eyes bright. "Famished."

"Then we'd better feed your beast."

The converted home had several rooms for dining,

each holding a variety of tables with seating for small and large groups. A pretty waitress with dark hair twisted into a bun at the nape of her neck greeted them.

"A reservation for MacLaren."

"Of course, Mr. MacLaren. Your table is ready."

They followed her to a booth in one of the smaller rooms. Dana slid over, hoping Mitch would choose to sit next to her rather than on the opposite side. Setting his hat upside down on the bench across from her, he sat down, grasping her hand in his.

"Whiskey for me and a margarita for the lady. No salt."

"I can't believe you remembered," Dana said, opening her menu.

"Are you kidding? I'm the one who had to carry you to the car the night we all went to Olivia's Hacienda and you split a large pitcher with Amber. And I took you home since you couldn't drive. I never saw anyone power down so many margaritas."

Dana couldn't remember much of anything about that night, except it had been the first time she'd accepted her attraction to Mitch and tried to drown it in alcohol. "I'll bet you couldn't wait to get rid of me."

He shrugged. "Eric had to get Amber home and no one else was around, so…"

"I see. So you played the martyr, sacrificing your time to take a lady home."

"Yeah, something like that." He didn't explain taking her home posed no hardship, nor did carrying her upstairs, holding her to his chest when she passed out after unlocking the front door. Laying her on the bed, he'd watched until certain she'd gone into a deep sleep, then left.

"Here you are." The waitress set down the drinks, took their order, then left as another server placed a heaping basket of chips and bowl of salsa on the table.

Dana picked up her glass and tilted it toward Mitch. "Thanks for the invitation."

"I'm glad you could make it up here on short notice."

They sat in silence, Mitch watching Dana's brows knit together as if trying to decide what to say.

"Go ahead, spit it out."

She whipped her head toward him. "What do you mean?"

"You're trying to decide if you should ask me a question." The corners of his lips curved up at the way her eyes widened. "Go ahead...ask."

"Well, I just wondered if you'd ever had a serious relationship."

The smile disappeared as a muscle flickered at his jaw, a grim expression clouding his face.

"You know, forget it. I had no right to ask."

He brought the whiskey to his lips and took a sip, letting it coat his mouth and warm his throat on the way down.

"One. In college. But I learned my lesson and won't let it happen again." He tossed back the rest of his drink and set the glass on the table.

"I'm sorry, Mitch. I shouldn't have asked."

He grabbed a chip, loading it with salsa, then putting it in his mouth, chewing slowly. Swallowing, he glanced at Dana. He'd been wondering the same about her.

"We were together three years. I met her in biology my freshman year. She was a sophomore and I thought we had something special. At least until I walked in on her and my best friend one night—in my bed. I tossed them both out, burned the mattress, and decided to never go down that road again."

Dana took a long sip of her margarita and sat back, speechless. She already knew he'd walked in on his mother and her lover, not once, but twice. Then to have his girlfriend repeat the betrayal. She took another sip and shook her head. The breakup with her boyfriend had been rough, but at least she'd never caught him in bed with another woman. Turning toward him, she speared him with a serious look.

"You're better off without that skank."

Mitch's mouth twitched until he couldn't contain a bark of laughter. "Damn straight. She was a skank." He motioned to the waiter for another drink and settled back, glad Dana hadn't made a big deal of it. "How about you? Anything serious?"

"One. Well, two if you count my high school boyfriend who broke up with me the night of senior prom."

"Ouch."

"I got over it. The serious relationship happened in Denver. I met him before Amber came to town and thought he could do no wrong. We talked of marriage, planned on it. Then one night he walked in after work, said he'd fallen in love with someone else, and walked out." She took a long gulp, almost finishing her drink. "I never saw him again."

Mitch rolled the glass of whiskey between his palms. "Seems we both have our reasons for not wanting to be in a relationship again."

Dana thought the same for a long time, but since she'd met Mitch, her hard stance on love had begun to soften. She needed to tighten it up again, and quick, before her feelings for him grew.

"The difference between us is someday I want a family—children and all the stuff that goes with it. So, at some point, I'll let myself fall in love again and marry. You're content to live alone with an occasional friend with benefits." Her stomached clenched, knowing she fell into that category with him.

For some reason her comment sent a chill through Mitch. He gripped his glass, staring into it, and wondering if his decision to deny himself any serious relationship still held true.

"These plates are hot," the waitress warned, setting their food down. "May I get you anything else?"

Mitch cleared his throat. "Uh...no, this is fine." He picked up his fork, scooped up a portion, and took a bite. The enchilada tasted like sawdust in his mouth.

"This is great. Here, you have to try it." She loaded her fork and held it out to him.

Mitch had never been one to enjoy sharing food, yet Dana shoving her fork in his face didn't bother him. Opening his mouth, he took what she offered, enjoying the mix of chiles and cheese with roasted tomato salsa.

"What do you think?"

He swallowed. "I can see why you like it."

"Well?"

"Well, what?"

"Don't I get to sample your enchiladas?"

He cut a section and held out his fork, letting her slide the corn tortilla, cheese, and chicken mixture into her mouth. Unable to tear his gaze away, he watched until she swallowed, then leaned down and kissed her.

"You had some sauce on your mouth," he explained as he pulled back.

"Thanks." A shiver rippled through her as she tried not to think of the future. Focusing on this one night, she finished her meal, looking forward to whatever time they did have together.

******

Mitch opened his eyes to slits as the moonlight slipped through the opening in the curtains. Reaching over, he found the space beside him empty, but still warm. He sat up and glanced around, not seeing her. Slipping into his jeans, he stepped into the dark hallway and walked toward the living room.

Dana stood in front of the large river rock fireplace,

wearing one of his t-shirts, her arms crossed. She stared up, focused on the oversized oil painting hanging above the mantel. It had taken him months to complete the landscape of the rugged mountains he saw each day through his studio window.

Stopping at her back, he wrapped his arms around her, feeling her shudder as he pulled her to his chest. "Do you like it?"

She relaxed against him, settling her hands on his. "I love it. This one and the landscape in the entry at Rafe's house are my two favorites. Do you have favorites?"

He lifted a hand to sweep soft strands of hair from her neck before letting his lips trail down the smooth column. "Hmmm...?" he breathed against her skin.

Dana tilted her head to the side, allowing him better access, then closed her eyes. They'd made love twice before exhaustion claimed them. Waking after midnight, she'd stared at the ceiling, listening to his measured breathing, and finally decided to search the kitchen for tea. Picking up her steaming cup, she settled onto the large leather sofa, studying the furniture and artwork, amazed at Mitch's talent. He never spoke of it and had yet to give her a tour of his studio. Perhaps it remained a part of his life off limits to anyone except family and close friends.

Sighing, she turned in his arms and looked up. "Your artwork. Do you have any favorites?"

"They're all special, but for different reasons." Huskiness from waking in the middle of the night, hungering for another round with Dana, lingered in his tone. "The one above the fireplace took the longest. I started it after graduating from college. I'd been absorbed in finishing the inside of the house as well as the studio and needed a distraction, something requiring effort and focus. It took several months before I was satisfied with it."

She rested her cheek against his chest and tried to stifle a yawn, wondering if the painting was therapy to help forget the betrayal of his college girlfriend. Or, maybe it came from sheer inspiration.

He lowered his arms and grabbed her hand. "Come back to bed, Dana. We still have a lot of time before sunrise."

******

"Are you ready?" Mitch swung up on his horse, glancing over his shoulder at Dana who sat a few feet away on a mare he'd acquired in early summer.

She nodded. "Ready." Shifting in the saddle to get comfortable, she thought of the previous night and the many times they'd made love. The soreness this morning served as a reminder, but she didn't care.

After breakfast they'd packed a lunch, Mitch deciding she needed to see the area from horseback rather than the passenger seat of his truck. As they walked toward the barn, she placed a hand on his arm.

"Am I ever going to see your studio?"

"It's not much. Are you sure you want to see it?"

"Absolutely," she smiled, excited to finally see where he created his beautiful artwork.

His lips tilted up at the corners. "All right. Come on."

He gave her a brief tour, explaining his pastimes and answering all her questions. Promising she could come back and study his work anytime she wanted, he took her hand and headed toward the barn to saddle the horses.

Riding side-by-side, he pointed out different landmarks, places he liked to ride, and relayed a little of the history of Crooked Tree.

"I don't know why Pop chose to come up here after the split with his father, Heath, and Jace. He doesn't share much, but I know he met Kade's mother not long after deciding this is where he wanted to settle and started to accumulate property. After she disappeared, he met my mother, bought more acreage, and built his house."

"*His* house?"

"Mother never wanted to stay here and didn't give a whit about the house. The life and town bored her." His lips thinned before a mirthless laugh escaped. "I think she kept having children to relieve the boredom."

The idea made no sense to Dana. "I doubt any woman would continue having children due to boredom."

"I don't know why they even married. She never wanted to stay, he never planned to leave." He glanced at her, seeing a smile spread across her face.

"Perhaps they were like us. Great chemistry." Her brows lifted a couple times, and she grinned at him. "Do you mind if we stop for a few minutes to stretch?"

His tried to wrap his mind around her comment. Yes, he and Dana had great chemistry, resulting in incredible sex. He also saw her as a friend, someone he could rely on to be honest and not play games. And he liked her, a lot. The thought she may have begun to crack his indifference bothered Mitch more than a little.

"Mitch?"

"Uh...sure. We'll stop under those trees." He pointed to a stand of junipers, still disturbed at how much he enjoyed her company.

Reining to a stop, he reached into his saddlebags, removing water and sandwiches while Dana spread out a blanket.

"Is this land part of the original ranch?"

"Yes. Over the years Pop bought as much property as he could afford, always intending each of his kids get a portion of it."

"It must have been hard to choose a spot. It's all so beautiful."

"Not for me. I knew for years this would be where I'd build a home, raise..." his voice trailed off as he realized what he'd been about to say. "Sean built his place last year and the others have their land picked out."

"Sounds like all of you plan to stay here and continue with the business."

"I don't see there's any reason for us to leave." He let his gaze wander over the expansive view, admiring his small herd of cattle in the distance. "It's paradise."

******

He led her on a different trail back to his house, pointing out two creeks, and the property line between his land and Sean's. As they rounded the last bend, both spotted a truck parked in front of the house.

"Guess we've got company," he muttered, looking at Dana, remembering her desire to keep their friendship quiet. "What do you want to do?"

"Why don't I put the horses away while you find out who it is?"

He nodded, already recognizing Sean's truck and hoping no one else waited inside. "I'll be out as soon as I can."

Dana took the horses into the barn, replacing the bridles with harnesses before starting on the saddles. She glanced over her shoulder a couple times at the sound of raised voices, then again when the truck engine roared to life. Not long afterward, Mitch came in and stopped beside her, his lips twisted into a hard line, jaw clenched.

"Sean just left. He drove out after he couldn't reach me on my phone." Mitch had turned it off during the ride, not expecting anything urgent. "Several of our bulls are down. Doc Wheaton is out there now. I need to go meet them."

"Of course. Do you want me to stay or try to get a flight back?"

"Stay. I shouldn't be gone too long." He wrapped an arm around her and hauled her to him for a ravishing kiss that left her breathless when he drew away. "I'll see you later," he whispered against her lips.

Watching Mitch leave, she couldn't help but wonder at all the problems befalling the company over the last weeks. Mitch mentioned the possibility of sabotage during their ride, not providing names, although she believed he had his suspicions. He focused on three groups—competitors, a former employee out for payback, or someone with a personal grudge against one or more of the owners. Most didn't know of the MacLaren acquisition, meaning, if it were a grudge, it would be against Rafe, Mitch, or one of his siblings.

She finished grooming the horses, then released them into the corral next to the barn, tucking her gloves into the back pocket of her jeans. Having no idea how long Mitch would be gone, Dana took a quick shower, not finding her sweats and t-shirt as she rummaged in her bag. Somehow she'd missed adding them.

Considering her options, which included wearing her slacks from the night before or her jeans from their ride, she opted to pull one of Mitch's t-shirts out of the dresser. The first one fell to her calves and the second had huge white skulls with crossed pistols on the front. Folding the two and setting them back in the drawer, she tried to pull out a third, but it hung up on something in the back of the drawer. Tugging slightly, it broke loose, and as she pulled the t-shirt out, a framed picture slid along with it.

Dana stared at the smiling faces of an older woman and a younger Mitch, arms around each other, the resemblance hard to miss—mother and son. She guessed it must have been taken in high school. Thinking back, Dana figured the timing to be after he'd caught his mother the first time and before finding her with the same man years afterwards. A picture like this should be on display to appreciate and share with others. The fact he'd tucked it away and probably hadn't looked at it in a long time told her a lot about his true feelings for his mother. The realization pained her. Betrayal was a hard pill to swallow.

Being careful to slide it all the way to the back, she closed the drawer and slipped into the long-sleeved camo shirt, the soft cotton feeling wonderful against her bare skin. Grabbing a book, she padded to the kitchen, searching the shelves, refrigerator, and freezer. After pulling salmon from the freezer, she set a box of pasta on the counter and began mincing garlic.

Another hour passed as she diced onions, sliced asparagus, and uncorked white wine to add to the sauce. Knowing it would all come together within thirty minutes after Mitch arrived, she picked up her book and settled into the oversized sofa. Within minutes Dana fell asleep to the ticking of the antique clock on the mantel.

Chapter Seventeen

"I still don't understand how four of our best bulls could fall ill within a few hours of each other unless it's the feed." Mitch walked Doc Wheaton to her truck, worry etched across his face.

"As I said, it could be the feed, although I believe it's unlikely. Let me do the tests. My guess is it's some kind of virus. I've already given them medication for infection. Obviously, none may be used in a rodeo until I figure out what's going on." Gayle set the samples in her truck and climbed into the driver's seat. "I'll call you as soon as I find out anything."

"What about the bull calves? Should we separate them?"

She shrugged. "If you want, but I don't believe whatever the adult bulls have is contagious."

Placing his hands on his hips, Mitch frowned as he watched her pull out onto the street. Her last words made no sense. Any vet worth their salt knew you isolated the sick bulls from those not infected with special care to isolating the calves.

"What did she say?" Sean stopped next to him.

Mitch continued to stare after her truck, remembering a comment that had always stuck with him. "Tell me the number one rule our prior vet always said to do about

216

infections?"

"Isolate the sick from the well animals. Why?"

"Gayle said she didn't believe it was necessary." Mitch turned toward the pens, walking toward Emilio and Fritz.

Sean hurried to catch up, wanting to figure this out between the two of them. "She was in a hurry, probably didn't register what you were asking."

Mitch stopped, not wanting to deal with what appeared to be a disconnect between him and the vet. "We need to separate them."

"Agreed. I'll speak with Emilio and Fritz. When will Wheaton get back to us on the test results?"

"She didn't say, but you can count on me calling her at first light tomorrow."

"Tomorrow's Sunday, Mitch."

"Do you think I care? We have thousands of dollars of sick bulls here. I want answers and don't care what day of the week I get them." Mitch stomped up the stairs to his office, slamming the door closed behind him as he grabbed his phone to call Heath, not wanting to bother Rafe during his recovery.

Ten minutes later he hung up, both agreeing not to say a word to Rafe, at least for a few more days when they'd have answers. Heath agreed with isolating the sick bulls and moving the calves to another location. They settled on moving the calves to Mitch's place, and bulls scheduled to compete, to Rafe's ranch. The remainder had already been relocated to the other end of the RTC stockyard. *At least the vulnerable calves would be at my*

217

place, Mitch thought.

The last had Mitch sitting up straight and checking his watch. It had been over five hours since he'd left Dana. Cursing under his breath, he raced down the stairs to the pens where Sean spoke to several of their men.

"I'm heading out. Keep me posted on any changes." Mitch dashed past without a backward glance, leaving the men to stare after him.

"What was that about?" Emilio asked Sean.

"I have no idea."

******

Mitch could see one dim light through the windows before pushing open the front door and stepping inside. Not seeing Dana, he checked the bedroom, study, then looked past the living room to the kitchen before spotting her curled up on the sofa. His face softened at the sound of her soft snores.

He sat beside her, careful not to break her deep sleep. After their workout last night, she deserved a long rest. Although he doubted his ability to keep his hands off her all night.

His stomach's growl reminded Mitch he hadn't eaten in hours. Grabbing a blanket, he laid it over her, then went searching for something to control his hunger until Dana woke up. Mitch came up short spotting the salmon and sliced vegetables in the refrigerator, and box of pasta on the counter. Looking at what she'd prepared, he had a pretty good idea of the plan for dinner.

His attempt at quiet failed about ten minutes into the cooking when he spotted Dana, still wrapped in the blanket, plodding up to him. Setting down the wooden spatula, he couldn't resist wrapping his arms around her for the kiss she offered. Breaking the kiss and stepping away, she looked around to see all the food laid out on the counter.

"How long have I been out?"

"I've been home maybe thirty minutes. I don't know how long ago you passed out." He picked up the spatula, sautéing the vegetables as the pasta boiled in a large pot. "About ten more minutes and we can eat."

"I know you make a mean breakfast. I had no idea your skills extended to dinner." She smiled, covering her mouth when it turned into a yawn.

"Lady, I have a lot of skills you don't know about." His knowing grin wasn't lost on Dana as he poured a glass of wine and handed it to her. "The next time you're here I want us to take a ride up into the mountains and camp at a spot I know. It's private with the best view of the stars and valley below."

She liked the thought, hoping he'd still want her in his life for many weekends to come.

******

Mitch grabbed Dana's bag and set it on the sidewalk outside the airport entry. The weekend had raced by faster than anticipated and they'd had to hurry to make her flight early Monday morning.

"Thanks for a wonderful time." Dana's smile lit her face as she looked up at him.

"With all the mess with the animals, I don't know when I'll get to Fire Mountain." Dana couldn't decipher the look that crossed his face. "Would you mind flying up here on Friday? I'll make the arrangements."

"I'd like that." She wanted to throw her arms around him, but they'd made a pact not to get too friendly in public places where someone might know him, and she was determined to keep her part of the bargain. Crossing her arms, Dana glanced behind her, wanting to catch her plane, but not anxious to leave. "Well, I guess I'd better go."

"Yeah. I'll see you Friday."

She caught her bottom lip between her teeth, then gave him a vague smile. "Friday."

Nodding, he turned his back to her, taking a few steps toward the truck, then spun around, taking long strides to catch her. Grabbing her shoulders, he turned her toward him, capturing her mouth in a deep kiss, not stepping away until he'd gotten what he wanted.

"Friday, Dana," he said again before turning toward his truck.

Her feet stayed planted in place until he'd pulled away, waving once as he drove off. Touching her fingers to her lips, she turned, took a deep breath, and walked toward the gate.

******

Juggling a coffee in one hand and his phone in the other, Mitch used his foot to push open the office door, surprised to see Sean, Skye, Sam, and Rhett waiting for him.

"I'll call you as soon as I hear anymore. Right." He hung up from the call and setting his coffee down, turned toward them, wracking his brain to recall if he'd missed something. "Am I late for a meeting?"

Sean shot a look at Skye, who sat forward in her chair, doing her best to hide a grin.

"Fritz took his aunt to the airport this morning."

"Yeah?" Mitch asked her.

"He saw someone who looked remarkably like you with a woman who bore an uncanny resemblance to Dana, kissing."

Mitch snorted, wondering what the odds were one of his employees would've spotted him saying goodbye to Dana. "And?"

"And was it? You and Dana?"

He crossed his arms, shooting them a hostile scowl that would've warned off anyone else. If he said yes, they'd want answers he couldn't give them, and he'd be betraying his promise to Dana. If he said no, he'd be lying.

The ringing of his phone provided a reprieve. He glanced at the others before answering the call.

"Pop, how are you feeling?" Ignoring their suspicious looks, he continued the conversation, avoiding a discussion of the sick bulls, then handed the phone to Sean. "He wants to talk about rodeo stats."

"Hey, Pop." Sean paced away, lowering his voice.

"Come on, Mitch. What's going on with you and Dana?" Samantha never pushed him about personal issues, at least not the way Skye did. More reserved, she tended to mind her own business. He also knew Sam liked Dana and had formed a bond with her. He hated shutting her down.

"I can't explain what Fritz saw, but listen up. My personal life is just that—personal. Now, are any of you in here to discuss business? If you're not, I'd suggest you get back to work."

He noticed the look of disbelief on their faces as they turned toward the door. None of them bought his brush-off.

"For what it's worth," Rhett said as he stepped into the hall, "I like her." He flashed Mitch a grin, then disappeared.

Sean hung up with Rafe and handed the phone back to Mitch. "He's a little concerned about the latest rodeo statistics. Nothing major. It was a good decision not to say anything to him about the sick bulls."

"I'm still waiting for a call back from Doc Wheaton. She never responded yesterday."

"Probably didn't have any news on the tests. We've done all we can for now, moving the calves to your place and our prime bulls to the pens behind Pop's house. Emilio and Fritz will go out to both places each day to check on the animals until we know what's going on."

Mitch kept his expression blank at the mention of relocating the calves to his place. He hadn't expected Sean and the other men to arrive unannounced early Sunday morning with the animals. He and Dana were in the shower when Sean pounded on his bedroom door, letting Mitch know what they were doing. At least the door had been closed so Sean couldn't see Dana's bag or clothes scattered about.

"Mitch, are you listening?"

"Sorry. I got distracted."

Sean leaned against the desk, studying Mitch and wondering when he'd fess up about Dana. He'd spotted her purse yesterday morning in the kitchen when he grabbed water for the men, but wouldn't push, knowing Mitch would talk about it when he felt like it, and not before.

"Do you think we should get another doctor out here?"

Mitch had been thinking the same. "A second opinion wouldn't hurt. Do you know of someone?"

"I haven't met him, but Fritz's cousin is a vet. Started a practice in town about a year ago. He'd keep it discreet."

"Get him out here. The sooner the better."

Both men turned as the office door opened and their receptionist poked her head in. "There's a call for you, Mitch, on the main line from a Matt Garner. Do you want me to take a message?"

"No, I'd better take this one." He looked at Sean. "Call the second vet and Doc Wheaton again. See if you can speed her up."

Sean nodded, closing the door as he left.

"This is Mitch MacLaren."

"We haven't met, but I'm—"

"I know who you are, Garner. What can I do for you?" He put the call on speaker and leaned back.

Matt cleared his throat before continuing. "First, I was sorry to hear about your father. I never met him, but I've known the MacLarens most of my life."

"That's what I hear from Cassie. Go on."

"Yeah, I'm sure you have. Anyway, Gage Templeton and I were talking over the potential of partnering on some rodeo contracts and think it's a good idea. At least to test out a couple times, see if there's a fit and we both make money."

Mitch leaned forward, resting his arms on the desk. "That's good news. What's the next step?"

"Well, we have a little hesitancy given what's been going on at RTC with the sick bulls, steroid tests, and all. We want to make certain there isn't something deeper going on we need to know about."

"Such as?"

"Look, Mitch. I'm going to spell out what I've learned and you tell me if I'm off base."

"Go on."

"Stock contracting is a small world. News travels fast and old news sticks with those who have a history in the sport. Gage asked me to poke around. What first grabbed my attention were some anonymous social media posts about RTC and your problems."

This got Mitch's attention. "Where were these posts?"

"On some association and bull contracting sites with blogs. Also on a few Facebook pages the contractors use for promotion. It's not often you see this stuff except on some known sites that specialize in degrading the business."

"Could you find out who posted them?"

"All we could find was they came from an Internet service provider who services Crooked Tree. Appears they may have been posted by someone right in your back yard. Unfortunately, we can't go further without dealing with law enforcement. I was able to find out some other information which might interest you."

"Let's hear it."

"You may not remember, but years ago, RTC bought out a failing stock contractor in Wyoming. Got it for a song. The owner had gotten deep in debt, had some other problems, and eventually drank himself to death, but not before unloading his business to RTC for cheap."

Mitch tried to recall Rafe saying anything about it. "May have been while I was still in school. Do you have names?"

"Dayton Hazard. He owned Hazard Stock Contracting."

"Now I remember. I don't know how much my father and his partners knew about the personal issues, but I do recall talk of them buying him out. Must have been at least ten years ago."

"Eleven. Here's what you need to know. According to the old timers I spoke with, Hazard lost all the money RTC paid him to a gambling habit, filed bankruptcy, and went through a divorce. The family was pretty much destitute, and from what I hear, blamed RTC for pushing Hazard to sell."

"Obviously Hazard hadn't been straight with his family," Mitch said.

"That's a given. Anyway, he had two daughters. One lives in Florida. The other lives in Crooked Tree and is a veterinarian. Gayle Wheaton."

Mitch cursed, slamming a hand on the desk. "That's our vet."

"Look, I found nothing to connect her to your problems, but I'm also not big on coincidences."

"Neither am I." Mitch thought of her advice about the calves and her not responding to his phone message. "I appreciate the information, Garner."

"Let me know if I can do any more checking for you. Sometimes an outside person can accomplish more with a few good questions."

"I'll keep that in mind. Let's plan to meet once we get through this situation."

"Sounds good. I'll wait to hear from you, Mitch."

The information Matt provided rolled around in Mitch's mind. He dragged a hand down his face, thinking back at all that had happened since Wheaton had become their vet. They'd lost thousands of dollars, dealt with doubts about their reputations, and looked to longtime employees as being behind the troubles.

Neither he nor Sean had suspected their problems might have been created by the person tasked with keeping the stock well. He wondered how far someone would go to seek revenge from a perceived wrong. *Pretty damn far*, he thought as he walked out the back door and down the stairs to the pens.

******

"It appears to me your bulls have contracted bovine respiratory syncytial virus, or BRSV. From reading the medication log, it doesn't look as if what Doctor Wheaton administered was the right antibiotic for this virus, which is possible since she didn't have test results when she administered the drugs." Veterinarian Dieter Palmer, Fritz's cousin, had come right over after receiving the request. "I've dealt a lot with this virus and I'm sure you're aware how quick it can spread, particularly in young bulls."

"I know you're in a tough situation, coming in and reviewing another doctor's work. We have to do what's right for the animals. What's your recommendation?" Mitch rested his hands on his hips, frustrated at the lost time and declining health of the bulls.

"Give me the okay to administer the right antibiotics."

"Done."

Mitch turned toward Sean, Emilio, and Fritz while the doc went to his truck for the medication.

"Doctor Wheaton is not to get anywhere near our animals. Send her to me or Sean when she shows up."

"Got it, boss." Emilio scratched his chin, shaking his head. "I still don't understand how anyone could carry a grudge this long, especially one so unfounded."

Before Doc Palmer arrived, Mitch had explained what he'd learned about Wheaton to Sean, as well as the potential for working with Double Ace in the future. Sean then told Emilio and Fritz about their suspicions, not mentioning Matt Garner's name.

"I have a call into Pop's partners. One of them might remember something." Mitch looked at Emilio. "Right now, you're the only one who worked here when they purchased Hazard."

"I've got to say I don't recall much other than the partners bought Hazard out for a great price. What I do remember is they didn't haggle with him. He set the amount and they snapped it up."

"Too good a deal to pass up," Sean commented, watching Doc Palmer as he administered the antibiotics. At least they'd contained the illness to a few bulls. The isolation should help keep the others safe.

"May have been the best acquisition they ever made. I may be wrong, but if you trace it back, I believe Absolute Devil eventually came out of that purchase. One of Hazard's bulls is the sire."

"All right, I've given them the antibiotics." Doc Palmer washed his hands, keeping his eyes on the bulls. "I'll be back first thing tomorrow to check on them. Unless you'd rather Doctor Wheaton continue from here."

"No," Mitch and Sean replied in unison.

"We need to speak with Wheaton and get an explanation before we make any firm decisions. For now, I'd ask you to stick with this until the bulls are well." Mitch grabbed his ringing phone, seeing the call came from Dana, and answered. "Hey. Hold on a minute." Taking a step toward the parking area, Mitch set his gaze on Palmer. "We want to keep this quiet until we know what happened."

"Understood." Doc Palmer grabbed his bag, shook hands, and left as Mitch disappeared in front of the building.

Mitch wished it were otherwise, but as soon as he'd seen Dana's name pop up on caller ID, a little of the weight he felt lifted. "How are you?"

"Good. I hope I'm not interrupting anything."

"No. It looks like we may be hiring a new vet. I'll explain all about it when I see you this weekend."

"That's why I called. Heath and Annie are having some shindig at their place Friday night. It's a combination work and family event, although I get the impression it's not entirely voluntary."

"You do what you need to do, Dana."

She could hear the disappointment in his voice and felt the same.

"I could still come up Saturday morning, unless you'd rather I not."

He didn't like either his dissatisfaction at the change

or his anticipation when she still wanted to fly up. His deal had been no attachments, just a casual relationship between friends, with benefits. Feeling anything more didn't fit his plan.

"I want to see you. I'll send the flight details."

"That's great. Should I bring up my own boots this time?"

He could almost see her smile through the phone. She'd used an old pair the weekend before, wearing two pairs of socks to fit the larger size.

"Probably a good idea. See you Saturday." He slid the phone back in his pocket, a grin still playing across his face as he turned around to see Sean standing a few feet away. "You got something you want to say?" he asked as the grin slipped from his face.

"Nope. I figure you'll tell me when you're ready."

"Well, I'm not ready." Mitch walked past him and into the office, prepared for the next fire he knew would be waiting.

Chapter Eighteen

Fire Mountain

"Are you going to tell me what's going on or keep me guessing?" Amber sat across from Dana, nursing a drink while Eric finished up his meetings.

"Neither, because there's nothing going on. I visited a friend last weekend and am doing the same this weekend. No great mystery."

Amber eyed her over the rim of the wine glass. "I've known you a long time, Dana, and there's something going on. I won't push, but if you want to talk about it, I'm here."

Dana studied the scotch in her glass, then set it down, her voice low. "Thanks."

"This doesn't have to do with a certain man in Crooked Tree does it?" Amber leaned forward when Dana's eyes shot to hers, then held a hand up. "Never mind. You'll tell me when you're ready."

Dana picked up the glass and took a sip. Last weekend had confused and excited her, resulting in a mix of mangled feelings she didn't know how to resolve. They'd known each other close to eight months, spent time together, learned a lot about the other, and became friends. In her mind, spending weekends in his bed wasn't hasty, but a natural result of her developing feelings and his unsubtle invitation.

She'd been careful to hide behind a shield of indifference most of the time, not sending out signals that might turn Mitch away. His response had been to pull her closer, showing a vulnerable side of himself he kept well hidden.

"He's overwhelming."

Amber almost missed Dana's whispered words. She didn't ask her to repeat them. Instead, she reached across the table, placing a hand on Dana's arm.

"Guard your heart with him. I don't want to see it broken."

Amber knew Dana had a mouthy, questioning side, the one exposed to strangers while she decided if they were friend or foe. She also had a private side, the one with a huge heart and generous nature.

Most were drawn to her easy smile, contagious laugh, and friendly manner. It hadn't been hard to see Mitch being taken with her—his night to her day. Amber just hoped he hadn't drawn her in too close, only to burn her and send her away.

Dana bit her lower lip and nodded. "I don't either."

******

Crooked Tree

"Please send her up." Mitch glanced at the men in the room. Sean and the sheriff sat across from him while

Emilio and Fritz leaned against a wall. Gayle had called the evening before, wanting to set up a meeting to go over the test results and her recommendations. It had given Mitch enough notice to pull everyone together.

There hadn't been time to mount a full investigation. Instead, the sheriff suggested confronting her with what they suspected to see if they could draw a confession from her.

The door pushed open as Gayle Wheaton walked in, coming to an abrupt halt. She recovered, plastered on a smile, and looked at Mitch.

"Good morning. Quite a group in here today."

Mitch heard the stammer in her speech and saw her hands shake as she took a step forward.

"Have a seat, Doc. We have some questions for you."

******

It took some time and a good many questions before she broke down, her confession pouring out at the evidence they'd compiled. Almost cocky, she smirked at how easy it had been with her access to drugs and ability to obtain the virus needed to infect the bulls. In her mind, RTC and the three partners had been the ones to drive her father to ruin, forcing him to sell his business for a fraction of its worth. The devastating loss of the business fueled his need for alcohol, ending in poverty for the family and his own death. She'd never looked beyond what her mother claimed were facts, working years to get inside RTC to inflict her payback.

Mitch almost felt sorry for her as the sheriff recited her rights and led her away, charges of malpractice pending as well as the loss of her license. A vet taking out her vengeance on animals negated all pity she might have gained from her story.

He and Sean had learned a hard lesson, one they wouldn't forget soon. Until Matt Garner's call, they'd believed her competent, even if she failed to advise them to move the calves. If it hadn't been for Matt's inquiries and reaching out to Mitch, they would have continued to experience increased illness, continued positive tests for steroids, and other problems. The issues would've been devastating to the business and ability to compete. At some point they would've looked at her more closely, but it could have been weeks or months before that happened, resulting in tens of thousands of dollars in losses.

They owed Matt for his help—the entire family did.

Now they had to focus on getting their animals well and explaining the facts to the rodeo committees, hoping to regain the trust they'd lost.

Mitch picked up the phone as the office emptied, deciding a thank you was in order before updating Heath.

"Matt, this is Mitch MacLaren..."

******

His plan to keep Dana at a distance was backfiring faster than it had taken him to come up with it. Work had

234

settled down as each bull regained its health and rodeo contacts became aware of the bizarre events which led to positive steroid tests. The one part of his life still in turmoil involved the only woman in years he couldn't seem to walk away from.

She'd flown up each weekend, and each visit she burrowed further under his skin and into his heart. Several times he'd made the decision to end it, save himself the pain of falling deeper under her spell. On each occasion he'd found a reason to wait. The truth was, he didn't want to face a weekend without her in his life. The same held true this morning as he grabbed her bag and walked her into the airport.

"I have an idea." Dana's sheepish grin accompanied her unconcealed enthusiasm.

"And that would be?" He set her bag down, his brows rising.

"Amber asked if I wanted to take some of my vacation time. I didn't think much of it at first, then thought...well..." her normal composure around Mitch slipped a bit when she saw the skeptical look.

"Thought?"

"I've never been to Las Vegas. And I thought, if you had some time, we could make plans to meet there." She waited, expecting him to shoot down her idea.

"When?"

"Maybe next weekend or the following. A Thursday through Tuesday, or whatever works for you." Dana held her breath. She didn't know why this meant so much to her. So far they'd kept their relationship quiet, going out a few times to places none of Mitch's friends frequented, taking long horseback rides, or riding his Harley with her on the back. She'd loved it all.

Mitch took his time deciding. Dana asked so little, flew back and forth each weekend without complaint, enjoyed everything, and left him wanting more of her each time her plane took off. But a vacation...together. Somehow it felt more permanent than what he'd intended when they'd made their agreement.

"Do you think we can stand each other for five nights and six days?"

She stepped closer, pressing a kiss to his lips. "If you get too ornery, I'm certain there are other amusements to entertain me in Vegas."

"Is that a fact?" he murmured, although his voice held an unsteady tone.

"Yep."

He checked the calendar on his phone. "This Thursday through Tuesday is best. The following week is a stock show I can't miss. You make the arrangements and I'll meet you there. Use my card." He'd given it to her weeks before so she could book the best flights.

"No. This one's on me." Hearing the announcement of her flight, she gave him a hug and kiss, flashed a brilliant smile, and took off through the security station. A quick wave and she disappeared around a corner.

Mitch felt trapped, as if he needed air and couldn't take a breath. Weekends had been perfect, enough time together without feeling smothered. A vacation would be more of a commitment. He'd already agreed to it, though, and wouldn't go back on his word.

Heading to his truck, he made a decision to enjoy the time with her in Vegas, then call it off. For him, it had come down to making her a permanent part of his life or cutting her out of it.

He couldn't push aside his fear of being swallowed up in a committed relationship, no matter how he felt about her. The risks were just too great. Besides, Dana had shown no signs of falling for him the same way he had for her. She'd been able to keep it light while he'd been captured, losing his heart during their time together. He needed to walk away now, end it before she met someone else and did the walking.

******

Las Vegas

"Come on, you'll love it." Dana grabbed his hand, pulling him toward the monster called Insanity at the top of the building.

He'd rather ride a raging bull any day than get on one of those mechanical thrill rides Vegas had become known for offering. They'd driven race cars the day before at the motor speedway, seen two shows, zip-lined, gambled, eaten until they couldn't hold another bite, and danced. Now she wanted to kill him on some insane piece of equipment.

"This is the last one, Dana. Any others and you're on your own."

If he survived the ride, which sat almost one thousand feet above the Las Vegas Strip, he'd never set foot on one again. In his mind, horses, motorcycles, and bulls seemed safer than these contraptions.

"I'll accept that. Let's go." Again, Dana led the way, getting in line and barely containing her excitement at the adventure to come.

Thirty minutes later they sat in a lounge, sipping alcohol-rich beverages. Most of the green tinge had faded from Mitch's face, replaced by a scowl Dana couldn't decipher. They had little else planned for their last full day other than supper and a late show. Ignoring the ride, he'd seemed off all morning, distant, as if something bothered him. Watching him stare at his drink, she wondered if he might be thinking their time together had run its course. She didn't want to ask, but needed to know what captured his thoughts.

"Is everything all right? You seem a little quiet." Dana did her best to look as if his answer didn't matter.

"Fine. Tired after all you've put me through." Mitch's deadline approached for calling it off, yet he couldn't bring himself to say the words. For the first time, he gained a measure of understanding of Matt Garner's decision to end it with Cassie by email. It may be seen as the coward's way out, but it sure held some appeal.

She wrapped a hand around his wrist, her bright blue

eyes searching his. "I had a great time. Thanks so much for coming here with me."

"I'm glad we did it. It's an adventure I won't soon forget."

******

He'd done his best during breakfast and again at the airport to tell Dana it was over. No matter how he tried, the words wouldn't come. It wasn't because he didn't want to see her, or didn't care for her. Instead, he'd fallen in love, which went against all his philosophies about relationships.

"Should I plan to fly up next weekend, or is that too soon?" Dana sat beside him in the waiting area. Her flight took off fifteen minutes before his and they didn't have much time.

"I have a stock show in Houston at the end of the week. Why don't I call you when I get back home?"

"I could go ahead and schedule flights for the following weekend, then give you the details when you call." Dana glanced at him, not liking the distant look in his eyes.

"Why don't you hold off until I know what's going on that weekend."

She felt as if a hole had opened in her chest and wouldn't close. He'd always been the one to make arrangements so they'd see each other every week. Either Vegas had been too much or it was all about to end.

"Sure, whatever you want. Just let me know." She stood as they announced the flight, picked up her bag, and faced him, plastering on the best smile she could. "I won't forget this weekend, Mitch, or any of them." Giving him a quick kiss on the cheek, she dashed off to the boarding line.

He watched until she disappeared, knowing his inability to call it off or agree to their next time together caused the hasty retreat. Taking slow, measured steps toward his gate, Mitch thought of the coming weeks and all he had to accomplish. The stock show, two rodeos he'd agreed to attend with Sean, a couple of dinner meetings, and a friend's birthday bash. He had a full plate with no room to squeeze in Dana. Then why did he already miss her?

Mitch had a lot to think about before he saw her again. He could jump in with both feet, go against all his sound reasons for avoiding a commitment and hope he survived, or go the route safest for his heart. Call it off and move on.

******

Crooked Tree

"Who was it?" Mitch glanced over his shoulder as he finished chopping salad and scooping it into a bowl.

"Someone named Dana," Lizzie said. "I introduced myself and she took off like a rocket."

"Shit," Mitch groaned, dashing to the door and throwing it open in time to see Dana make a U-turn in the drive. "Dana, wait!" He ran after her, calling again until he saw the brake lights flash once then stay on. Stopping on the driver's side, he signaled for her to roll down the window. "Where are you going?" he asked, his voice winded.

Dana pushed the door open, almost slamming it into Mitch in her hurry to get out. She stepped up to him, a finger stabbing into his chest as her voice rose in anger.

"You're a rat bastard, MacLaren. We agreed to tell each other when it was over. You agreed and so did I. I come all the way up here to find Lizzie settling in. How could you do this?" She swiped at tears, trying to steady her voice and control the emotions which flared at the sight of Lizzie.

"Dana—"

"No, I don't want to hear your excuses. I knew from the start you didn't want anything permanent. All you had to do was let me know it was over. Couldn't you have done that one thing for me?" She gulped in air as her anger began to lose steam. Crossing her arms, her shoulders slumped as she turned toward the car. All this time she'd counseled herself over and over not to fall in love with Mitch, not to expect a relationship he couldn't provide.

It had been three weeks since their time in Las Vegas. Now she knew why he'd pushed away her suggestions to visit, feeling humiliation heat her face at her impulsive move of flying up unannounced.

"Dana, wait." He caught up with her, placing his hands on her shoulders and pulling her back against his chest. The feel of her in his arms felt so right after being apart. "It's not what you think." Unable to resist, he brushed a strand of hair aside and bent his head, placing kisses along her neck, causing her to stiffen.

"Don't." She tried to step away, but he held her to him.

"Lizzie came by to introduce me to someone." He turned Dana around, locking his gaze with hers and seeing so clearly in her eyes how she felt—misery, pain, and love. The knowledge rocked him. How had he not seen it before now? Her cool manner and quick goodbyes made him believe he'd been the one to be twisted into knots about their relationship. Now he knew she was in as deep as him. Clearing his throat, he continued. "She brought by her fiancé. Lizzie's getting married in a few weeks."

Dana opened her mouth to speak, then closed it. Feeling like an idiot, she pushed away, trying to compose herself and decide how best to withdraw from an embarrassing and hurtful situation.

"I don't want to intrude, so I'll get going. Have a good time tonight." Once again she turned away.

This time Mitch let her slide into the car before he stalked in front of it, his face set as he crossed his arms and planted his feet shoulder width apart, making it impossible for her to leave.

She leaned out the window, glaring at him. "Move."

He didn't budge.

"Dammit, Mitch. Move."

Again he acted as if he didn't hear her. She slammed her hands on the steering wheel. All she wanted was to leave and head back home, even if it meant staying in a cheap motel tonight. If he'd invited her to spend the weekend, it would be different. But he hadn't asked her to come in a long time. It didn't take a genius to figure out he'd gotten over their time together.

Dana inched the car forward, hoping to make him believe she wouldn't stop if he continued to ignore her. He let her get within inches of his legs, never shifting his stance.

"Turn off the engine, Dana. You're not going anywhere." His voice held a cool finality she'd never heard.

She slumped into the seat, knowing she'd lost whatever battle they fought. Turning the key, she shut off the engine as he opened the door, holding out his hand.

"Come inside. Meet Lizzie and her fiancé, have supper with us, then we'll talk."

******

"Look, I understand, it's over. You don't need to go into detail or make excuses. I'm not some dense bimbo who wants to hold on to something that isn't there." She paced around his living room, speaking as if to herself without glancing at him. Her arms moved through the air as she spoke, at times seeming to boost her anger.

Lizzie and her fiancé had stayed a little longer than Mitch wanted, finally leaving a few minutes earlier. He'd grabbed Dana's hand, leading her into the living room, seeing the distress on her face, but not getting a chance to talk as she launched into her diatribe.

Mitch leaned against a wall, crossing his arms, taking a deep breath as she continued to rant.

"I told you all you had to do was tell me and I'd be history. No drama, just gone. Stuff happens, don't you think I understand that? I'm not even asking why—"

She didn't notice him push from the wall until he snaked an arm around her and pulled her to him, a hand covering her mouth as her eyes opened wide.

"Be quiet, Dana," he whispered, waiting as she took several deep breaths. "Are you done? Nod if you are and I'll remove my hand."

She nodded, frozen in place as he let his hand drop.

He turned toward the sofa, sitting on the edge, and stretching his legs in front of him. "C'mere," he said, crooking a finger at her.

"I..."

"Right here." He patted the seat next to him.

Taking a few tentative steps, she didn't shift her gaze away, even as she lowered herself beside him. He reached over and took hold of a hand, pulling it onto his lap and letting his thumb make slow, seductive circles on her palm.

"First, I have every intention of continuing to see you. In fact, my intention is to see a lot more of you, not less."

He took a breath, working up his courage, praying he had the nerve to go through with this. The one point keeping him focused was the look in Dana's eyes earlier. He'd bet his ranch she loved him.

"Second, there's a reason I didn't make time to see you the last few weeks."

"What reason?" She looked away, letting her attention focus on the carpet.

His grip on her hand tightened. "You were becoming an addiction. One I didn't need or want, so I purposely pushed you away, tried to extricate myself from how I felt."

She turned to face him, her lips parting. "And did you, extricate yourself?"

"No," he breathed out. "And that brings us to number three." He shifted, running a finger down her cheek and across her lower lip, then leaned over and pressed a kiss to her mouth.

"I love you, Dana. There's no way I'm ever letting you go." He slid off the sofa to one knee and looked up into her stunned face. "Breathe, baby, so I can continue."

She sucked in a deep breath, then exhaled, her heart beating so hard she thought it would explode.

"Good...real good." He took a breath of his own, then said what had lodged in his throat for weeks. "Marry me, Dana."

She covered her mouth to stifle a scream as tears formed in her eyes. Her throat worked, but nothing would come out.

"I know it won't be easy and we'll fight, push each other's buttons. We'll figure out work and where we'll live and..." his voice trailed off as she placed a finger on his lips, then removed it, sliding off the sofa next to him and wrapping her arms around his neck.

"Be quiet, Mitch." She kissed him, then leaned back. "I love you, too, and yes, I'll marry you."

Epilogue

Fire Mountain
One week later...

"I can't believe you got married without telling anyone." Amber still hadn't forgiven Dana for her and Mitch's quick trip to a justice of the peace in Crooked Tree.

Dana shifted her drink to the other hand, looking across Heath and Annie's expansive front yard at her husband, joking with Sean, Kade, and Cam. They'd married on Monday, then she'd flown back to Fire Mountain, asked Annie if it would be out of line to have a reception at their home on Saturday to celebrate the marriage. Annie had almost strangled her with a hug before picking up the phone and making arrangements. Amber may never forgive her for being the second person in Fire Mountain to know of the wedding and not the first.

"He refused to have a big wedding and wouldn't let me fly back without putting a ring on my finger. I told you as soon as I could."

"After you told Annie." Amber crossed her arms, still hurt Dana hadn't called.

"Look, I didn't get back in town until late Monday night. You were out of town until Tuesday night. I had to speak with Annie right away since Mitch had already arranged for the company jet to fly him down here on

247

Friday. You and I had a meeting at eight o'clock Wednesday morning. I showed you the ring the minute I walked in the door." Dana took a breath, exhausted at all the apologies she'd had to make during the week after their quick marriage. At least her parents had been able to fly in Friday night. Her brothers, all in Special Forces, were deployed and couldn't make it, but she'd been able to get word to them.

"And a honeymoon?"

Dana smiled, remembering how he hadn't let her out of his bed all day Saturday after her acceptance of his proposal Friday night. They'd taken a long horseback ride Sunday, finding shelter from a threatening storm under a stand of pines, and made love before falling asleep, nestled in each other's arms. He'd woken her with feather-like kisses, whispering of his love before showing her in slow, explicit movements how he felt.

"We want to go to Hawaii in a couple months when both our schedules clear up. I still don't know what I'm going to do about my job." And that seemed to be her biggest problem. She loved her job working with Amber out of the company headquarters and hoped to work out a way she could continue.

"Don't worry about it. Heath told me he and Mitch talked this morning." Amber gave her a smug smile. At least she'd been able to surprise her.

"They did? How come Mitch didn't tell me?"

"Possibly because you and Annie have been knee deep in today's reception, plus entertaining your parents. I'm so glad they made it. Your dad sure has hit it off with Heath, Jace, and Rafe." Amber loved Dana's family, including her brothers.

"My dad hits it off with anyone, as long as they aren't anti-military," Dana grinned. Her father was career Army, and her mother retired as an Army nurse. Between them and her brothers, she'd been surrounded by military most of her life. She turned her head toward Mitch, seeing him wave her over. "Guess I'll spend some time with my husband." The word still felt odd on her lips. She gave Amber a hug before crossing the lawn.

"I was telling these wusses about the ride in Vegas. They don't believe I went on that monster. Set them straight for me, sweetheart." Mitch slipped an arm around her shoulders and pulled her close, placing a kiss on her temple.

"Mitch did finish the ride, although it took him two whiskeys to lose the green color in his face," she laughed. "He did do great on the race car track. Beat me by what, a couple seconds?" She glanced up at him, her eyes glistening.

"About that." Mitch took a sip from his drink, watching a truck pull up and someone he didn't recognize get out. "Does anyone know who that is?"

The others looked in the direction he pointed, trying to make out the new guest.

"Ah, shit," Eric blurted out, then glanced at Dana. "Sorry, it's just that it's someone we haven't seen in a long time."

"Who?" Mitch asked.

"Matt Garner," Cam answered. "He hasn't come around since the breakup with Cassie. I wonder who invited him."

"I did." Mitch dropped his arm from around Dana and took off toward Matt, who'd stopped when Heath walked up to him. Getting close, he could pick up a little of what was said, none good.

"You're right, Heath. I have no excuse for how I acted and can only hope someday Cassie, and you all, will forgive me." Matt shoved his hands in his pockets, noticing another man walk up.

"Matt Garner?"

"That's right."

"Mitch MacLaren. It's a pleasure to finally meet you. I'm glad you could make it." He stuck out his hand, turning his face toward Heath. "I told you how Matt's digging saved us regarding Gayle Wheaton. He and I spoke again about joint contracts a couple days ago. When he mentioned being in Fire Mountain this weekend, I invited him to the reception."

Heath nodded, but said nothing.

"Good to meet you, Mitch." Matt accepted Mitch's hand before turning back to Heath. "Look, I don't want to cause problems. Why don't I leave you to the party? I'll give you a call, Mitch."

Matt turned toward his truck, taking a few steps before Heath called him back.

"Hold on, Matt. At least say hello to Annie. Eric and

Jesse couldn't make it, but most everyone else is here. Just be careful around Cassie."

Matt lifted a hand to his nose, rubbing gently. "Don't I know it."

"Come on, I'll clear a path for you," Mitch offered. He knew there might be hell to pay for inviting him, but it had felt right to extend the invitation. They'd talked, Matt letting it slip how he'd like to rebuild his bridges with the MacLarens. Mitch thought there would be no better time to start than today. The look on Cassie's face as she stormed toward them told him he might have been wrong.

"What the hell are you doing here?" Cassie stopped a foot short of coming toe-to-toe with Matt.

"Hello, Cassie. Mitch invited me."

She shifted her gaze to Mitch, but said nothing.

"Fine. You've come, now you can leave." She fisted her hands at her sides, itching for one more shot at him.

"You know what, Cass, Mitch invited me and Heath asked me to stay. I guess you'll have to deal with it."

"Why you..." She reared her arm back, but this time Matt's hand shot out, catching her at the wrist, and pulling her toward him.

Matt didn't say a word as he drew her closer, to within inches of his mouth, and stared down at her, noticing her nostrils flare and bright eyes shoot daggers at him.

"You may have caught me once, Cassie, but never again."

*****

Join me in the continuation of the MacLarens of Fire Mountain Contemporary series with No Getting Over You, Book Seven

Will pride and self-preservation control their future? Or will one be strong enough to make the first move, risking everything, including their heart? Start reading **No Getting Over You** to find out!

If you want to keep current on all my preorders, new releases, and other happenings, sign up for my newsletter: https://www.shirleendavies.com/contact-me.html

A Note from Shirleen

Thank you for taking the time to read **Hearts Don't Lie**!

If you enjoyed it, please consider telling your friends or posting a short review. Word of mouth is an author's best friend and much appreciated.

I care about quality, so if you find something in error, please contact me via email at shirleen@shirleendavies.com

Books by Shirleen Davies

Contemporary Western Romance Series

MacLarens of Fire Mountain

Second Summer, Book One
Hard Landing, Book Two
One More Day, Book Three
All Your Nights, Book Four
Always Love You, Book Five
Hearts Don't Lie, Book Six
No Getting Over You, Book Seven
'Til the Sun Comes Up, Book Eight
Foolish Heart, Book Nine

Macklins of Whiskey Bend

Thorn, Book One
Del, Book Two
Boone, Book Three

Historical Western Romance Series

Redemption Mountain

Redemption's Edge, Book One
Wildfire Creek, Book Two

Sunrise Ridge, Book Three
Dixie Moon, Book Four
Survivor Pass, Book Five
Promise Trail, Book Six
Deep River, Book Seven
Courage Canyon, Book Eight
Forsaken Falls, Book Nine
Solitude Gorge, Book Ten
Rogue Rapids, Book Eleven
Angel Peak, Book Twelve
Restless Wind, Book Thirteen
Storm Summit, Book Fourteen
Mystery Mesa, Book Fifteen
Thunder Valley, Book Sixteen
A Very Splendor Christmas, Holiday Novella, Book Seventeen
Paradise Point, Book Eighteen,
Silent Sunset, Book Nineteen
Rocky Basin, Book Twenty, Coming Next in the Series!

MacLarens of Fire Mountain

Tougher than the Rest, Book One
Faster than the Rest, Book Two
Harder than the Rest, Book Three
Stronger than the Rest, Book Four
Deadlier than the Rest, Book Five
Wilder than the Rest, Book Six

MacLarens of Boundary Mountain

Colin's Quest, Book One,
Brodie's Gamble, Book Two
Quinn's Honor, Book Three
Sam's Legacy, Book Four
Heather's Choice, Book Five
Nate's Destiny, Book Six
Blaine's Wager, Book Seven
Fletcher's Pride, Book Eight
Bay's Desire, Book Nine
Cam's Hope, Book Ten

Romantic Suspense

Eternal Brethren, Military Romantic Suspense

Steadfast, Book One
Shattered, Book Two
Haunted, Book Three
Untamed, Book Four
Devoted, Book Five
Faithful, Book Six
Exposed, Book Seven
Undaunted, Book Eight
Resolute, Book Nine
Unspoken, Book Ten
Defiant, Book Eleven, Coming Next in the Series!

Peregrine Bay, Romantic Suspense

Reclaiming Love, Book One
Our Kind of Love, Book Two
Edge of Love, Book Three, Coming Next in the Series!
Find all of my books at:
https://www.shirleendavies.com/books.html

About Shirleen

Shirleen Davies writes romance—historical, contemporary, and romantic suspense. She grew up in Southern California, attended Oregon State University, and has degrees from San Diego State University and the University of Maryland. Her passion is writing emotionally charged stories of flawed people who find redemption through love and acceptance. She now lives with her husband in a beautiful town in northern Arizona.

I love to hear from my readers!

Send me an email: shirleen@shirleendavies.com
Visit my Website: https://www.shirleendavies.com/
Sign up to be notified of New Releases:
https://www.shirleendavies.com/contact/
Follow me on Amazon:
http://www.amazon.com/author/shirleendavies
Follow me on BookBub:
https://www.bookbub.com/authors/shirleen-davies

Other ways to connect with me:

Facebook Author Page:
http://www.facebook.com/shirleendaviesauthor
Twitter: www.twitter.com/shirleendavies
Pinterest: http://pinterest.com/shirleendavies
Instagram:
https://www.instagram.com/shirleendavies_author/

Made in the USA
Middletown, DE
20 September 2023

38867855R00149